THE JORDAN FILE
AN AUNT BESSIE COLD CASE MYSTERY
BOOK TEN

DIANA XARISSA

Copyright © 2023 by DX Dunn, LLC

Cover Copyright © 2023 Tell-Tale Book Covers

Cover Photo Copyright © 2019 Kevin Moughtin

ISBN: 9798367778977

All rights reserved.

No part of this publication may be reproduced, distributed, or transmitted in any form or by any means, including photocopying, recording, or other electronic or mechanical methods, without the prior written permission of the publisher, except as permitted by U.S. copyright law. For permission requests, contact diana@dianaxarissa.com

The story, all names, characters, and incidents portrayed in this production are fictitious. No identification with actual persons (living or deceased), places, buildings, and products is intended or should be inferred.

First edition 2023

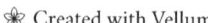 Created with Vellum

CHAPTER 1

"I can't believe we are actually doing this," Bessie Cubbon said as her friend, Andrew Cheatham, drove them towards Ramsey.

"I'm surprised we've managed to keep the unit quiet for as long as we have," Andrew replied.

"The island does thrive on skeet."

Andrew laughed. "Such a wonderful Manx word."

"It doesn't just mean gossip. It can also mean to have a quick look at something."

"I didn't realise that, but my Manx is seriously limited."

Bessie laughed. "I've taken the introductory Manx class more times than I want to admit, and my Manx is also seriously limited."

A few minutes later, Andrew drove the car into the Seaview Hotel's large car park. He found a space near the entrance, and the pair walked together from the car into the hotel's gorgeous lobby.

"Good afternoon," Sandra Cook said from behind the reception desk. "How are you today?"

"I'll be better after our meeting is over," Bessie said a bit glumly.

Sandra gave her a sympathetic smile. "I was surprised when Mr. Coventry told me who is joining you today."

"Needs must," Andrew told her.

"Mr. Coventry has put you in the penthouse meeting room today," Sandra added. "And he's sent up some extra-nice treats for you as well."

Bessie smiled. "Jasper knows this meeting won't be pleasant."

"I've done everything I could to make it as pleasant as possible," Jasper Coventry said as he walked out of the office behind the reception desk.

He walked around the desk and pulled Bessie into a tight hug. "It isn't too late to sneak out the side door," he whispered in her ear.

Bessie laughed. "It's a tempting thought, but we simply need to get this over with."

Jasper nodded. "In that case, I'll escort you to the penthouse. Your guest has already arrived."

"Of course he has," Bessie muttered as she took the arm that Jasper offered.

"Surely you have better things to do than this," Andrew said to Jasper as they waited for the lift.

"Our summers are very busy, but that doesn't mean that I don't still personally look after my favourite guests," Jasper replied. "What's the point in owning a hotel if you can't take care of your friends?"

"We appreciate everything you do for us," Andrew told him.

"I don't do much, really," Jasper protested.

"You usually spoil us with amazing food for our meetings, even though we're only paying for biscuits and coffee," Andrew countered.

THE JORDAN FILE

"You're doing very important work, and I feel privileged that you've chosen to have your meetings at the Seaview."

The lift doors opened, and the trio stepped inside the car. As the doors slid shut, Jasper spoke again.

"I'm just sorry that we can't provide rooms for Charles and Harry during the summer months. I hope they are enjoying staying on the beach in Laxey instead."

"They are, very much, actually," Bessie told him. "They both appreciate the extra space that the cottages on the beach provide, but I think they're both looking forward to moving back here in September. I believe they both miss your restaurant and room service."

"And housekeeping," Andrew added. "There's something wonderful about being out all day and coming back to a clean room and a freshly made bed."

Jasper grinned. "We do our best," he said as the lift doors opened again. The threesome walked together to the conference room, where the door was standing open.

"Here we are," Jasper said. "If you need anything, please let me know."

Andrew nodded. "As ever, thank you."

Bessie looked at Andrew and then took a deep breath before she walked into the room. Andrew followed and the door slowly shut behind them. The man sitting at the head of the table looked up from his plate, which was stacked high with cakes and biscuits.

"Ah, I was starting to think no one was actually coming," Dan Ross said with an unpleasant smile.

"We're early," Andrew pointed out as he headed towards the table in the back of the room.

"But I'm a busy man on a deadline," Dan countered. "I have a dozen other places to be, a dozen other stories to write. As the *Isle of Man Times's* only investigative journalist, I'm always in very high demand."

Andrew slowly filled a plate with small cake pieces and biscuits before he replied. "If you need to reschedule our conversation, we can do that," he offered.

Dan shook his head. "I'm just eager to get on with it. I've already written the outline of the article on the cold case unit, but I need a lot more information to finish the piece."

Andrew poured himself a cup of coffee and then walked to the table. Bessie watched, wondering where he'd sit, as he typically sat at the head of the table himself. Andrew didn't hesitate before putting his plate and cup down as far from Dan Ross as he possibly could. Bessie quickly made her own selections from the delicious treats on the table before putting her plate next to Andrew's. She poured herself some tea and then sat down next to him.

"We may as well get started," Dan said. "I know you're a retired Scotland Yard Inspector who has written a number of books about investigative techniques. Why start a cold case unit now?"

Andrew popped a piece of cake into his mouth and chewed it slowly. He washed it down with a sip of coffee before he spoke. "I think it's probably best if we wait to begin until everyone is here," he told Dan.

Dan frowned at his watch and then shrugged. "I hope I don't get called away for anything more important."

I hope he does, Bessie thought. She nibbled on a biscuit as the clock slowly ticked its way to two o'clock.

"I thought the meeting was due to start at two," Dan said at one minute past the hour.

Andrew nodded. "I can't imagine what's keeping everyone," he said as he got to his feet. He crossed to the door and pulled it open.

"Ah, there you are," he said to someone just outside of the room.

"We were, um, just chatting," Hugh Watterson said as he

walked into the room. Doona Moore and John Rockwell were right behind him. Charles Morris and Harry Blake followed the others. As Andrew shut the door behind them, the new arrivals all gathered around the table at the back of the room.

"I do have other things to do," Dan said loudly as he watched everyone fill plates.

"Don't let us keep you," Doona replied.

Dan flushed. "I was invited to be here today."

"And we're all, um, willing to speak with you," John told him. "Just give us a moment to get some coffee or tea and we'll join you."

Five minutes later, everyone was sitting around the table sipping drinks and eating biscuits and cake. Andrew sighed and then cleared his throat.

"As you all know, I've invited Dan Ross from the *Isle of Man Times* to join us today. He's going to be writing an article for the newspaper about our very unique cold case unit. He'll be including a brief biography of each of the members and a short explanation of the work that we do. We will not be discussing any of the cases we've considered as a unit with him, though."

Dan frowned. "I thought maybe you could tell me about just one, sort of as an example of the kind of work that you do."

Andrew shook his head. "I'm afraid we can't do that. I will tell you that we consider cases ranging from missing persons to murder and that we've had a much higher success rate than I was expecting us to have when I formed the unit. I'm afraid that's all I'm going to say on the matter."

Dan looked as if he wanted to argue, but after a moment, he simply opened his notebook and made a note. Okay, where do you want to start?" he asked.

"Introductions?" Andrew suggested.

"Sure," Dan replied. "I already know most of you, but let's pretend I don't."

"I'm Inspector Andrew Cheatham. I'm retired from Scotland Yard. I spent a good deal of my career investigating homicides and other serious crimes. Once I'd retired, I found that I missed the work. A chance conversation with a friend about a cold case got me thinking about starting some sort of cold case unit. This unit is the end result of that random conversation, really. I called in a few favours to get the people who I wanted in the unit, and we've been meeting for several months now."

"And how does the unit work?" Dan asked as Andrew stopped for a sip of his drink.

"We consider a single case each month," Andrew replied. "We start by going through the entire case file from the initial investigation and then work our way through any available updates. Once we've had a chance to consider everything, we send questions to the man or woman who is currently in charge of the investigation. He or she goes back and talks to witnesses again and again, taking new statements and sharing those statements with us."

"And have you managed to solve any cold cases thus far?" Dan asked.

We've solved them all, Bessie thought, shoving a bite of cake into her mouth before she could say anything out loud.

"We've been more successful than I'd expected us to be," Andrew told him. "And that's all I'm going to say on the subject."

"My sources suggest that you're being sent cases from all over the world now," Dan said. "My sources told me that lots of people are hoping for your help."

Andrew nodded. "Units like this one are unusual, and there are unsolved cases in every police jurisdiction in the world. There is nothing a police inspector wants more than to solve every case in which he or she is involved, even if that means bringing in outside help."

"But you wouldn't be as in demand if you weren't so successful," Dan suggested.

"When I first set up the unit, I emailed about a half-dozen inspectors I knew from around England," Andrew told him. "Those inspectors sent back over a dozen cases that they were interested in having our unit consider. That was before we'd even had our first meeting. Yes, we've had some success, but even if we hadn't solved a single case, we'd still have plenty of cases to consider."

"So why only one a month?" Dan asked.

"Because that's what we can reasonably manage," Andrew told him. "Three of the members of the unit are retired, but all three of us do other consultancy work, too. Two of the members are still working full-time in policing. Another has other business concerns."

"And then there's Bessie," Dan said with a smug smirk.

Bessie flushed. "What does that mean?" she demanded.

"As I understand it, you've never held down a paying job," Dan said. "Surely you have time to look at more than one case a month."

"But we're a unit," Andrew told him. "We work together on each case, one at a time, in a way that's working for us. At the moment, I don't have any plans to change anything."

"How frustrating for the many men and women who need your help," Dan said.

Andrew shrugged. "We do what we can."

Dan nodded. "Right, so you're retired from Scotland Yard, and so are two others in the unit." He looked at Harry. "Harry Blake, I understand you were a homicide inspector, specialising in the most horrific of crimes."

Harry frowned. "That isn't how I would put it," he said stiffly.

"How would you put it, then?" Dan asked.

"I was a homicide inspector, full stop," Harry told him.

"But you did do more than your fair share of investigating the most awful of crimes," Dan said.

"I investigated the cases I was assigned to investigate."

"And now that you've retired, you work with this unit and also as a consultant, working to find serial killers, as I understand it."

"That isn't exactly correct," Harry told him.

"Which part?"

Harry shook his head. "For the purposes of your article on the cold case unit, clarification is unnecessary."

Dan frowned at his notebook. "But I want the article to be as accurate as possible."

"I'm Charles Morris," Charles interrupted. "I'm the other retired inspector in the unit."

Dan stared at Charles for a moment and then looked down at his notebook. "As I understand it, you're an expert at finding missing people," he said eventually. "Is there much demand for that in a cold case unit?"

"We've considered cases that involved missing people," Charles replied.

"And Charles is an expert investigator, no matter what the crime," Andrew added.

Dan made a note. "Were you able to find any of your missing people?" he asked.

"No comment," Andrew said quickly. "I told you we aren't going to discuss the cases we've considered."

"Now that I have the basics, tell me more," Dan said. "I want my readers to get to know you as people. Tell me about your wives, your children, your hobbies, what you like to do with your spare time. Harry, I believe you own a small vineyard in France. Tell me about that."

Harry looked surprised and then slowly shook his head. "No comment," he said tightly.

Bessie exchanged glances with Doona, who looked as surprised as Bessie felt. *How did we not know that Harry owns a vineyard in France?* she wondered. She sat back in her seat, feeling frustrated that, even after several months, she still didn't feel as if she knew Harry or Charles very well.

"Charles, tell me about Mandy," Dan said.

"I don't know what you're talking about," Charles said flatly.

"Of course you do. You must remember Mandy Montgomery. She was your first missing person case, wasn't she? And your first serious girlfriend, as I understand it," Dan said.

"I'll be back when he's gone," Charles said as he got to his feet. He left the room before anyone could reply.

"Wow. I didn't mean to upset him," Dan said, sounding smugly pleased with himself. "Maybe one of you could answer my questions. You all must have heard the story by now."

Bessie frowned. Maybe some of the others had heard the story, but she certainly hadn't.

"I believe you were told that we are going to limit today's interview to brief introductions and a discussion of the cold case unit," Andrew said. "If you can't keep on topic, we can end the interview right now."

"Does that mean you don't want to talk about your wife and children?" Dan asked. "As I understand it, your wife's death wasn't entirely straightforward. I've been told that some of your children still haven't forgiven you for what happened to her."

Andrew opened his mouth to reply and then snapped it shut again. He took a long, deep breath before he spoke again. "As I said, we'll keep the conversation on the cold case unit or end this right now."

Dan shrugged. "Okay, then, what else can you tell me about Charles?"

"I believe he told you everything you need to know," Andrew countered. "You need to meet everyone else in the unit."

Dan laughed. "Oh, but I know everyone else. Police Inspector John Rockwell, who runs the police station in Laxey. His wife died under mysterious circumstances, too, but I don't suppose anyone wants to talk about that, either."

John gave Dan a cool smile. "Sue and I were divorced, and she was married to another man when she passed away while on her honeymoon. If you have questions about what happened to her, you should talk to her second husband."

Dan nodded. "I'd love to talk to him. I've left dozens of messages for him at every number I have for him, but he never rings me back."

"He's a busy man," John said flatly.

"As I understand it, he's actually doing some good work in Africa," Dan said. "Even if he is mostly hiding there so that he doesn't have to answer any questions about what happened to Sue."

John shrugged. "He's been interviewed by the local police."

"And you've been left to raise two teenagers on your own," Dan said. "How is that going?"

"I love my children and I'm very proud of them. They've had a lot to deal with over the past few years and they're both doing great, regardless," John said.

"It must help that you have a new woman in your life, too," Dan said. "Although I'm not clear on exactly when you and Doona became involved. Someone told me that you were already sleeping together before your divorce."

Doona inhaled sharply. "Your someone gave you the wrong information," she said angrily. "Not that it's any of your business."

John put a hand on her arm. "I believe we're meant to be talking about the cold case unit," he said.

Andrew nodded. "And if you ask more inappropriate questions, this conversation is over," he warned Dan.

Dan grinned at him and made a note. "Okay, so John Rockwell is currently with the local island police. So is Hugh Watterson." He nodded at Hugh. "How does a lowly constable end up on a cold case unit with four inspectors?"

"Hugh is an excellent investigator who is working hard to advance his career," Andrew replied. "He also works well with the other members of the unit, and I was delighted to be able to include him when I was putting the unit together."

"You're in school, aren't you?" Dan asked Hugh. "I'm surprised you have time to study, with a wife and a baby at home. Between work, school, and this unit, you must never see baby Alice."

"Her name is Aalish, and I spend as much time with her as I possibly can," Hugh told him. "And none of that is relevant to today's conversation."

"Of course, I'm not certain how Doona can run a UK holiday park from the island, either," Dan said. "What a wonderful inheritance, though. Such a shame your husband had to die so tragically in order for you to become a millionaire."

Bessie was surprised when Doona chuckled.

"I'm beyond caring what you think of me, Dan," she said.

"Does it worry you that John Rockwell only started chasing after you once you became rich?" Dan asked.

Doona and John exchanged glances and then they both burst out laughing.

11

"Not at all," Doona said eventually. "But you're wandering off topic again."

Dan looked down at his notebook. "That just leaves Bessie, of course. Elizabeth Cubbon, known as Aunt Bessie to nearly everyone. Age unknown, or rather, unacknowledged, although my sources suggest that she's well past eighty. Bessie is another one who inherited a fortune, decades ago now. She used the money to buy herself a cottage on Laxey Beach and she's been living there ever since. What must it be like to inherit so much money that you never have to work a day in your life? I'd love to find out."

"You've already worked for a great many years," Bessie pointed out.

Dan frowned. "You know what I mean."

"Again, you're quite far away from what we're meant to be discussing," Andrew said. "If you don't have any more questions about the cold case unit, we can wrap this up."

"How do you choose which cases you consider?" Dan asked.

"I get emails every day from people who want us to consider cases. I read brief summaries of every case that is suggested, and then I request more information on the ones that interest me. I try to focus on cases where I feel things were missed, but, at the end of the day, it often just comes down to random choice," Andrew explained.

Dan looked up from his notebook. "You make all of the selections?"

"I have so far. That may change in the future," Andrew told him.

"Tell me something about the case you're going to be considering this month," Dan suggested.

Andrew shook his head. "I'm afraid I can't do that."

As Dan opened his mouth to reply, loud music began to

play somewhere. Dan frowned and pulled out his mobile. He glanced at it and then sighed. "I need to answer this," he said as he got to his feet and headed for the door. He started talking immediately.

"What?" He sighed.

"Right now?" Dan made a face. "Surely someone else…"

"I'll be there in ten minutes," he said after a brief pause.

"I have to go," Dan said as he turned around before he reached the door. He dropped his mobile into his pocket and then walked back to pick up his notebook and pen. "Thank you for your time thus far. When can we continue?"

"I think you have everything you need for your article," Andrew replied. "If you have any additional questions, why don't you just ring me?"

Dan clearly wanted to argue, but his mobile began to ring again before he could speak. Frowning, he pulled out the device and headed for the door.

"I'll ring you," he shouted over his shoulder as he left the room, his mobile to his ear.

CHAPTER 2

"That was unpleasant," Bessie said as the door swung shut behind Dan.

"I'm just glad he was called away," Doona said. "I couldn't have taken many more of his rude questions."

"I was about ready to end the interview," Andrew said. "He wasn't supposed to ask about anything other than the cold case unit once we'd completed basic introductions."

"Surely you didn't expect him to do as he'd been asked," Bessie replied.

Andrew chuckled. "No, of course not, but I didn't expect him to be quite as rude as he was."

"You don't know Dan very well," Bessie told him.

"I can't wait to see what he puts in the paper," Doona said. "The headline will probably be something about how we all have mysterious pasts or some such thing."

"Dan will find a way to sensationalise anything," Bessie sighed.

Andrew pulled out his mobile and sent a quick text. "Charles is on his way back," he said. "Then we can talk about this month's case."

"Is it murder again?" Hugh asked.

"Yes, and maybe no," Andrew replied. "It's a strange one this time."

"They've all been strange," Doona said.

"Okay, it's a stranger one this time," Andrew told her with a chuckle.

"Sorry about that," Charles said sheepishly as he entered the room. "I should know better than to let someone get to me in that way."

"I should have made Dan leave after that, really," Andrew said. "But the interview was arranged by the man with whom I'm working at Scotland Yard. He was quite keen for us to share some information with Dan."

"Why?" Harry asked.

Andrew shrugged. "Apparently, Dan has been ringing Scotland Yard regularly, demanding information. He's also managed to learn just enough to be difficult. We're hoping that, having told him about the unit and its work, Dan will write his article and then forget all about us."

"If we don't tell him anything about our cases, he should get bored pretty quickly," Doona said.

"And we won't be telling him anything about our cases," Andrew replied. "It's been difficult keeping quiet about the unit up until now. At least we no longer have to try to sneak in and out of the Seaview."

"So tell us about this month's case," Charles said. "I hope it's a really interesting one, the type that Dan would love to hear all about and won't."

Everyone laughed as Andrew pulled a stack of envelopes out of his bag.

"I'm going to give you all your copies of the case file now," he said. "You may want to look at the crime scene photos in a moment or two."

I never want to look at crime scene photos, Bessie thought as

Andrew handed her an envelope. As much as she was pleased to be part of the unit that had solved a number of cold cases, she didn't enjoy some aspects of the job. Having access to police files had sounded quite exciting when she'd first agreed to join the unit, but she hadn't realised just how awful crime scene photos could be.

"This month's case comes from Cheyenne, Wyoming," Andrew told them.

"That sounds very Wild West," Doona said.

"It's the capital city of the state of Wyoming, but its population is only around sixty thousand people," Andrew replied.

"That seems very small for a US state capital. Mind you, it seems small for a US city as well."

Andrew nodded. "As you can imagine, murders don't happen very often in Cheyenne, and this particular case was out of the ordinary in other ways, too."

"Tell us everything," Charles said.

"Leo and Anna Jordan had been married for almost fifty years when their bodies were discovered in their home by their older son, Roy," Andrew began. "He found them in the early afternoon on the fifth of July 1996."

"Not that long ago, then," Harry said.

"It wasn't that long ago," Andrew agreed. "We don't usually consider cases from only five years ago, but this one really interested me."

"What happened to Leo and Anna, then?" Bessie asked.

"If you look at the first crime scene photo, what do you think happened to them?" Andrew asked.

They all opened their envelopes and pulled out the file folders inside. It took Bessie only a moment to find the relevant photo.

"They just look as if they're sleeping," she said, feeling relieved.

Andrew nodded. "And that's what Roy thought when he

first entered the house. He thought his parents had simply overslept. When he couldn't wake them, he rang his brother, Robert. When Robert arrived, he insisted on ringing the police."

"Why?" Charles asked. "It looks very much as if they simply died in their sleep."

"While Roy was waiting for Robert to arrive, he found a note written by his father," Andrew explained. "A copy of the note is at the front of your files."

Bessie flipped back and slowly read through the note as Andrew read it aloud.

"'We've been talking about this for months, and we've agreed that tonight is the night. I'm going to help Anna first and then end my own life. Please don't feel sad. This is the right decision for us now. Roy and Robert, we love you both always. We'll meet again in a better place. Leo.'"

"Leo killed Anna and then himself?" Doona asked.

"It certainly appeared that way," Andrew told her. "Autopsies revealed that they'd both been given fatal injections of the same deadly substance. You can read the details in the file, but it was something that Leo had had access to at his workplace. He would have been fully aware of just how lethal it was."

"Were they both dying of some sort of horrible disease?" Doona asked. "Or were they in tons of debt and unable to pay their bills?"

Andrew shook his head. "Leo was seventy-three and Anna was seventy. They both had a few minor health complaints of the sort that come with age, but neither was suffering from anything serious. They were both able to get around well, and from all accounts, were still enjoying life. They had sold their large family home about ten years previously and bought the smaller property with cash. From what I've been told, they had plenty of money in the bank, and they both had decent retirement incomes as well."

"Was one of them having an affair?" Charles asked.

"Not as far as the police have been able to determine. Roy told them that as far as he knew, neither of his parents had ever cheated. He said he'd always thought that they were truly devoted to one another."

"So much so that Leo killed Anna," Doona said.

"Did he, though?" John asked.

"Obviously, that's the question the police want answered, or one of them, anyway," Andrew said. "The autopsies were able to determine that Anna did die first, at least half an hour before her husband."

"So why are we considering the case?" Harry asked. "There must be more to it than what you've told us so far."

Andrew nodded. "There were a few minor inconsistencies with the murder-suicide story. It's still a possibility, but something felt off to Jake Montana. He was the detective in charge of the investigation."

"Jake Montana?" Doona echoed. "Does he rope cattle in his spare time?"

Everyone laughed.

"He's a solid investigator who has been in charge of more than a few murder investigations in his day," Andrew told her. "And his gut instinct on this one was that it wasn't what it appeared to be."

"If it wasn't murder-suicide, then it was murder times two," Harry said.

"That's what Jake suspected, anyway," Andrew told him.

"So who wanted Leo and Anna dead?" John asked. "And where did the note come from?"

"Jake narrowed down the suspects to five people," Andrew said. "He's convinced one of them killed both Anna and Leo and set it up to look as if Leo had killed Anna and then himself. Five years later, he's concerned that he may have narrowed his suspect list too quickly. He wants us to go back through all of his notes from the initial investigation to see if he missed any obvious suspects."

"There must have been dozens of other possibilities," Charles said.

"I'll let you see what you think after you read the file," Andrew told him. "I will say that I can see exactly why Jake narrowed his list to the five people on whom he focussed."

"And he's certain that both of the Jordans were murdered?" Doona asked.

"He's as certain as he can be, but he's lacking clear evidence," Andrew replied. "He's hoping he'll be able to find more if he can work out exactly what happened to the couple the night they died."

"Tell us about the suspects, then," Doona suggested.

"I'm just going to go through them quickly and then leave you to read the police reports," Andrew said. "These are in no particular order, by the way. Jake told me that he's moved each suspect up and down his mental list a dozen or more times, and that he's never been convinced that any of the suspects was more likely to have been the killer than any of the others."

"That's odd," John remarked. "I nearly always have a suspect or two that seem more likely than the others when I'm investigating a crime."

Andrew nodded. "It is odd to have five very different suspects and not have one stand out. It will be interesting to see how you all feel about the suspects once you've read the reports."

Bessie turned the page in her notebook and got ready to write. Everything Andrew was about to tell them would be in the file, but she often found that it was useful to take notes during Andrew's summaries. Then she could refer back to her notes on the suspects while she was reading the file.

"The first suspect on the list is Roy Jordan," Andrew said. "As I said earlier, he was the couple's older child. He was forty-eight when his parents died."

"He found the bodies," Doona said. "How long had they been dead when he found them?"

"At least twelve hours," Andrew replied. "But Roy had been at the house the previous day, celebrating the Fourth of July at a family party."

"So Leo and Anna had a party the day before they died?" Bessie asked.

Andrew nodded. "The Fourth of July is an important holiday in the US, and apparently the Jordan family celebrated with a large family party every year."

"Just how large was the family party?" John asked.

"Actually, it was more of a small family party the year in which they died," Andrew replied. "Roy gave Jake a brief history of the celebration, which used to include their entire extended family and a great many friends and neighbours as well. In the last few years before their deaths, though, the party had become smaller. Some of the family had moved away or passed on, and they were inviting fewer friends and neighbours each year."

"So how many people were actually at the party the day before the bodies were found?" Harry asked.

"About a dozen people attended, but that was spread out over the course of the entire day," Andrew explained. "Apparently, people were welcome from midday until midnight, although from what Jake could determine, the last guests left around eleven, after the fireworks."

"They set off fireworks?" Bessie asked.

Andrew shook his head. "From their garden they were able to see the fireworks display that was set off at a nearby park every year. Leo and Anna used to set out chairs so that everyone could sit and watch the show at the end of the evening."

"Who was the last to leave the party?" Harry asked.

Andrew shook his head. "I'm going to let you all read about the party and the guests," he told him. "I shouldn't have answered as many questions as I have, really. I want you to approach the file with an open mind."

"But now we're all curious about the party," Doona said with a laugh. "It seems likely that someone from the party killed them, after all."

Andrew sighed. "According to several witnesses, everyone who stayed to watch the fireworks left together as soon as the show was over. One of the neighbours offered to help clear everything away, but Leo told him not to bother. When they all left, Leo was stacking away folding chairs in the garage, and Anna was putting all of the leftover food away."

"So someone went back later to kill them, assuming they truly were murdered," Bessie said thoughtfully.

Andrew nodded. "That's how it appears, anyway."

"How quickly would the poison have worked?" John asked. "Is it possible that they were jabbed during the party and that it took time for the poison to actually kill them?"

"According to the lab report, the poison would have started having an effect almost immediately, and it would have killed them within minutes," Andrew replied.

Bessie sighed. "Tell us about the suspects quickly so that we can all go home and read the reports."

Andrew laughed. "I'm trying, but you all keep asking me questions."

"You said Roy was a suspect. Did he have a reason to want his parents dead?" Doona asked.

"By all accounts, he got along reasonably well with his

parents," Andrew told her. "But he did inherit quite a lot of money when they died."

"And money is a very powerful motive," Charles said.

"What about the other brother? Is he a suspect? Did he inherit a fortune, too?" Bessie asked.

"Robert is also on the short list of suspects," Andrew confirmed. "And yes, he and Roy inherited equal shares in the estate. Of the two, Robert needed the money more than Roy."

"Oh?" Bessie replied.

"Robert was forty-one when his parents died," Andrew began.

"Seven years younger than Roy?" Doona asked.

Andrew nodded. "You'll find that many people felt that he'd been rather spoiled by his parents, and especially by Anna. According to Anna's medical records, she'd suffered through several miscarriages after she had Roy and before she had Robert."

"So when she finally had him, she spoiled him," Doona concluded.

"While Roy had followed in his father's footsteps, earning degrees in chemistry and biochemistry and then going to work at the same laboratory where Leo worked, Robert dropped out of university after a year and appears to have moved from job to job fairly frequently. He was working part-time as a nightclub bouncer when his parents died."

"Only part-time?" Harry asked.

"His parents were supplementing his income by paying his rent and his car loan for him," Andrew explained. "Even so, he was heavily in debt when they died, starting with a small fortune in student loans that he'd taken out for his single year at university."

"I hope he's doing better now," Bessie said. "I assume we'll get updates on everyone at the next meeting."

"You will," Andrew agreed.

"If his parents were paying his bills, surely he had a good reason for wanting them alive," Doona said thoughtfully.

"I suppose that depends on the size of his inheritance," Charles said.

"One of the party guests – Scott Bailey, actually, about whom we will talk more later – claimed that he overheard a heated discussion between Robert and his father," Andrew said. "Scott said that he heard Leo say that he wasn't going to be paying any of Robert's bills any longer. Robert denies that any such conversation ever took place."

"Interesting," Charles said, making a note.

"And you'll have to read the rest in the file," Andrew said. "Let me tell you a bit more about Scott Bailey. He was in his mid-forties when Leo and Anna died. He worked in retail management, managing a women's clothing shop. He lived next door to the Jordans, and he and Leo had been fighting for over five years about an extension that Scott wanted to add to his house."

"That's a long time to fight with a neighbour," Hugh said.

"Did you say he was a guest at the party?" Harry asked.

"He was." Andrew's answer was surprising. "While Scott was angry that Leo kept objecting to his requests for permission to extend his house, he still maintained an outwardly friendly relationship with the Jordans, or so he claimed in his interview. He went to the party for a few hours, but went home before the fireworks."

"Did something happen that made him leave early?" Doona asked.

"No, but he was having his own fireworks-viewing party in his own back garden," Andrew told her. "He was one house closer to the park, so he felt he had a better view, anyway. He'd invited a few of his friends to come and have a drink and watch the fireworks with him."

"And then they left just in time for him to sneak over and murder his neighbours," Doona suggested.

"Maybe," Andrew replied. "The next suspect is Russell Newton. He worked with Leo before Leo retired."

"In the laboratory that stocked deadly poisons," Charles said.

Andrew nodded. "Russell was in his mid-sixties when Leo died. According to his statement, he and Leo were close friends, but according to Roy, who also works at the same place, Russell and Leo barely got along."

"Was Russell at the party?" Bessie asked.

"He was, although he didn't stay until the end of the evening," Andrew told her.

"So he and Leo must have been somewhat friendly towards one another," Doona said.

"Roy suggested that Russell was better friends with Anna than with Leo," Andrew replied.

"Better friends?" Hugh echoed. "Was he suggesting that his mother had an affair with the man?"

"You'll have to read the statement for yourself and see what you think," Andrew said. "Jake didn't see it that way, and he actually spoke to Roy, so it seems unlikely. As I said, see what you think when you read the statement. Our last suspect is Colleen Allen. Colleen was forty-six when the Jordans died. She's the office manager for a large dental practice in the city. She and Roy were a couple for about ten years, starting in the early eighties."

"They never married?" Doona asked.

Andrew shook his head. "They did not and, by all accounts, they ended things amicably. Colleen remained friendly with Leo and Anna, and she always spent the Fourth of July with them, often bringing the current man in her life with her."

"That's just odd," Hugh said.

Andrew chuckled. "It is somewhat unusual."

"Why was she a suspect?" Bessie asked. "What possible motive could she have had for killing Leo and Anna?"

"Jake speculated that she was hoping to get back together with Roy, but she knew that his parents would object. They were still friendly with the woman, but they didn't think she was right for Roy. That's just speculation on Jake's part, though. I got the impression that he didn't care for Colleen and was just looking for any possible motive for the woman," Andrew replied.

"So she should be at the bottom of the list of suspects," Bessie said.

"See how you feel after you read the file," Andrew replied. "That's all I'm going to say for right now."

"I'll go and start reading, then," Harry said as he got to his feet.

The door was still closing behind him as Charles got up to follow him out. "See you all tomorrow," he said as he went.

Bessie slowly began to pack up her things as Hugh walked back to the table and began to fill a takeaway container with some of what was left. She was just thinking about doing the same thing when someone knocked on the door. A moment later, Jasper walked into the room.

"I hope I'm not interrupting," he said.

"Not at all. We've just finished," Andrew assured him.

"Excellent. I was wondering if I could have a quick word with Bessie before you go," Jasper replied.

"Of course," Bessie said, trying not to worry about the unexpected request.

CHAPTER 3

Hugh quickly finished filling his box and then headed for the door. "I'll see you all tomorrow," he said before he exited.

Doona and John weren't far behind. They both gave Bessie quick hugs before they left.

"I can get out of your way," Andrew said as Jasper paced back and forth in front of the table at the back.

"You can stay," Jasper told him. "I probably should have asked Inspector Rockwell to stay, too, but I'd rather not involve the police."

"You do know that I'm with the police," Andrew reminded him.

"But you're retired, and out of your jurisdiction, I believe," Jasper replied.

Andrew nodded. "But I will ring John if I think that's the right thing to do."

Jasper sighed deeply. "It may be the right thing to do, but it's difficult for me to consider doing it. I think of the men and women who work here as part of my family, and I hate the thought of any of them getting arrested, even if they have done something, um, well, less than legal."

"Less than legal?" Bessie echoed. "What's happened?"

Jasper sat down next to Bessie and then got to his feet again. As he returned to pacing, he inhaled slowly. "One of our guests rang me this morning. He and his lovely wife stayed with us last month. It was their twenty-third wedding anniversary and they wanted to have a short holiday somewhere close to home. They wanted it to feel special, though, so they booked a week with us. They walked on the beach each day and toured some of the island's historical sites. Each evening they had dinner in our restaurant and then drinks in the bar."

"And?" Bessie asked after Jasper fell silent.

"And they just received their credit card bill and found over a dozen charges that were not theirs," Jasper said in a rush.

"Ah," Andrew said. "Someone stole their credit card information while they were on holiday."

"Exactly, and it seems very likely that that someone works for me," Jasper said miserably.

"Sit down," Bessie suggested. "Sit down and take a deep breath. What makes you think the information was stolen here?"

Jasper sank into the seat next to Bessie's and sighed. "According to the guest, he used a very specific card while he was here, one that he only uses very occasionally. He used it to pay for the room and for his meals in the restaurant and nothing else."

"What about the other charges?" Andrew asked. "Were they at shops on the island?"

Jasper shook his head. "They were all over the place, including some charges in Spain and France. The guest is rather unhappy with his credit card company for not noticing the unusual activity, but apparently he'd told them that he was going to be travelling, and the charges were simply automatically approved."

"So whoever stole the credit card information probably sold it to someone who was able to use the details in multiple locations at once," Andrew said.

"That's what our guest was told when he reported it to the police," Jasper told him. "Apparently, such things are not uncommon. The man I spoke to from the police said that I should look very closely at my staff because it's likely that one of them was behind the theft."

"How awful," Bessie said.

"It wasn't the first time," Jasper said in a low voice. "I've had a few other, similar complaints in the past few days. I didn't really take the first one seriously, because it was from a man who was a very unpleasant guest while he was here. I assumed he'd simply rung to complain yet again and that his card had probably been stolen elsewhere. To be fair, he did admit that he'd used the card in dozens of places on the island and while travelling. The details could have been stolen anywhere."

"Were there just two complaints?" Andrew asked.

Jasper shook his head. "There were three. As I said, I didn't take the first one seriously. The second one came yesterday. One of our regular guests, a man who visits the island at least twice a year, rang. He wasn't ringing to complain, though, he simply thought I should know that I might have a problem. Again, though, he'd used the same card here as he'd used while travelling to get to the island and also in the weeks before and after his visit. I told myself that it wasn't anything to worry about."

"Until the third person rang," Bessie said.

"Exactly," Jasper replied gloomily.

"Did all three of the guests use the cards in question to

pay for their rooms and for meals in the restaurant?" Andrew asked.

Jasper nodded. "We let guests charge their meals in the restaurant to their room and then add the charges to their accounts at the end of their stays, but none of the three men in question actually did that. All three used their cards in the restaurant at least once during their stays."

"And they all used the same cards that they'd used to pay for the room?" Andrew asked.

"Yes," Jasper replied.

"So who has access to the credit card information behind the reception desk?" was Andrew's next question.

"There are three people who work behind the reception desk," Jasper told him. "Any of them could have gone through the paperwork behind the desk and copied down the credit card information from any account. I trust all three of them, though. You both know Sandra, I believe."

Bessie nodded. "And I refuse to believe that she's involved in stealing anything in any way."

"I agree," Jasper said. "But then, I'd say the same about everyone else that I employ."

"Tell me about the other two people who work reception," Andrew said as he pulled out a notebook and pen.

"Sandra works days, mostly, and she's here nearly every day. Mindy Holloway works a mix of days and nights. She has an odd schedule, but she prefers it that way."

"What else can you tell me about Mindy?" Andrew asked.

Jasper shrugged. "She's a lovely young woman in her mid-thirties. She's single, and she enjoys travelling in her spare time. We make rooms available to our staff during our quieter months, and Mindy always takes advantage of every opportunity to come and stay in one of our rooms or suites. She's been working here for about three years now, and I trust her completely."

"And the third person?" Andrew asked.

"Colin Payne has been with us for over two years. He works nights, usually from six until midnight. After midnight, one of our security team sits behind the reception desk to assist any guest in need, but we don't allow guests to check in or out between midnight and eight."

"What if someone is leaving on the early ferry?" Bessie wondered.

"They can check out the night before they are due to leave," Jasper explained. "Our security staff has enough to worry about without having to deal with checking people in and out. It's not usually an issue, but if necessary, I have been known to get up at four in the morning to check someone out."

"So the security staff shouldn't have access to credit card information," Andrew said.

"They definitely don't. Before Colin leaves at midnight, he locks the office and shuts down the computer. Sandra switches it back on when she arrives at eight and she unlocks the office as well."

"How good is the lock on the office?" Bessie asked.

Jasper grinned at her. "It's excellent, actually. And all of the paperwork inside the office is kept in locked cabinets. We also have security cameras inside the office that are monitored throughout the night. If someone breaks in, he or she will be seen by someone else from the security team."

"What else can you tell me about Colin?" Andrew asked.

"He's forty and married with three kids under the age of six. His wife stays home with the kids, and he loves working here because he's close to home. He used to work at one of the large hotels in Douglas, but his wife is from Ramsey and refused to move there, so he's much happier here."

"And you trust him completely?" Bessie asked.

"I do," Jasper agreed.

Bessie sighed. "If the card information wasn't stolen from reception, then it must have been stolen from the restaurant."

Jasper nodded. "And the restaurant has a much larger staff, of course. I pulled all of the receipts from when those three guests were here and discovered that there were only four members of the restaurant team who came into contact with all three of them."

"Four? That seems a lot," Bessie said.

"All three guests ate in the restaurant on several occasions during their stay," Jasper told her. "And most of our restaurant staff work only a few days a week. I thought it would be more, really."

"Tell me about the four, then," Andrew said, turning the page in his notebook.

"Peter Christian is the assistant manager of the restaurant," Jasper said.

Andrew nodded. "We've met," he said.

"Ah, yes, he was involved in the incident with Sandra, wasn't he?" Jasper asked. "He and Sandra are quite delightfully in love with one another, and I'm certain neither of them would do anything illegal, but he was working in the dining room on occasions when all three of the guests involved dined there."

"And that would have given him access to their credit card information?" Bessie asked.

"When guests use a credit card, they give the card to their waiter or waitress and the waiter or waitress takes the card to the manager on duty for processing," Jasper explained. "We do that because we had an incident many years ago in a hotel I was managing in England where one of our waiters was putting through charges that included very generous tips for himself. By having a manager put the charge through, we're able to ensure that the correct amount is being charged for each transaction."

"So Peter had access to all three cards," Bessie said.

"As did three others," Jasper said. "Sherry Brady works breakfast and lunch most days, and she waited on all three of our guests during their stays."

"I know her mother," Bessie said.

Jasper laughed. "That shouldn't surprise me."

"The family lives in Ramsey now, but Sherry's mother grew up in Laxey," Bessie explained. "If I'm remembering correctly, Sherry has three sisters and two brothers. She's the baby of the family."

"She is," Jasper agreed. "And she's still struggling to decide what she wants to do with her life. She's taking some classes at the local college while she tries to determine what she really wants to do."

"She must be in her mid-twenties by now," Bessie said.

"She is, and she's been working here for over a year," Jasper told her. "In the last month or so she's started talking about moving across, though. One of her sisters just had a baby, and Sherry's been considering going over to act as a nanny for her."

"I'm sure her mother would hate to see her go," Bessie said.

"Apparently her mother is considering going with her," Jasper replied.

"Interesting," Bessie said. "I assume you trust her, too."

Jasper sighed. "I trust all of my staff. I wouldn't hire them or continue to employ them if I didn't."

"Who is next?" Andrew asked.

Jasper frowned. "Al Clarke. He's in his early sixties and is semi-retired. He works here only a few days a week, usually working breakfast because he's naturally an early riser. He used to work in banking, and his pension covers his expenses. He works here to get a bit of extra spending money. He, um, likes to bet on sporting events, but only in a small way."

Andrew looked up from his notes. "Gambling can become a problem over time."

"Yes, I know, but Al is sensible about it. As I said, he works here to get the money he uses for betting. He wins fairly regularly, too, because he spends a lot of his spare time studying the sports and the teams before he places his bets."

"And he waited on all three guests?" Bessie asked.

"He did, always at breakfast," Jasper told her.

"Is Al married?" Andrew asked.

Jasper shook his head. "He was married briefly many years ago. Apparently his wife ran off with another man after just a few months, and he's never seen or heard from her again. As far as he knows they are still legally married, but he told me that after that he didn't think women were worth the bother."

"I wonder if it's worth trying to find the missing Mrs. Clarke," Andrew said, making another note.

"That leaves only one other possible suspect," Bessie said.

Jasper winced. "I hate to think of my people as possible suspects," he said.

"But you do need to get to the bottom of what's happening," Andrew told him.

"I know, but it's very difficult. The last of the people who waited on all three of the guests in question is Todd Hoffman. He works the dinner shifts on weekends, which can be very profitable."

"Tell us about Todd, then," Andrew said.

"He's thirty-five and he lives with his mother, who has a few small health concerns that make it advantageous for her to have someone at home with her. She has a sister who comes and stays with her on Friday and Saturday evenings while Todd is at work, but, according to him, that's more because she gets lonely than because of her ill health. He's able to leave her for several hours at a time if he needs to, which means he can cover other shifts here in a pinch."

Bessie frowned. "Is his mother Joney Hoffman?" she asked.

Jasper nodded. "I should have expected you to know her."

"I don't know her, not really, but I know of her," Bessie countered. "I do know her sister Betty. She's been looking after Joney since they were children. Joney has some sort of heart condition, but I don't know how serious it is. I do remember Betty telling me that Joney's doctors told her not to have children, but then Joney fell pregnant anyway."

"Is Todd an only child, then?" Andrew asked.

"Oh, yes," Bessie replied. "As I recall, Joney had a very difficult pregnancy, and I believe she was told a number of times that the baby wasn't going to survive. When Todd finally arrived safely, she was delighted."

"What about Todd's father?" Andrew wondered.

"He and Joney had been married for only for a few months when she fell pregnant," Bessie told him. "He was from somewhere across, and while she was on bed rest, he went back to wherever he'd come from, ostensibly so that he could make some extra money to help pay for everything the baby might need."

"And then he never came back," Andrew guessed.

"Oh, no, he did come back," Bessie told him. "But he came back with his girlfriend, who was about seven months pregnant when they arrived on the island, just a few weeks after Todd's birth. Joney refused to let him see Todd, and he and his girlfriend left a few days later."

Jasper grinned. "I've heard the story from Todd's perspective. It's interesting to hear it another way."

"What did Todd say?" Bessie asked.

"Let's just say that his version is filled with hatred for his father and for the woman with whom his father became involved while Joney was pregnant," Jasper said.

"I may be misremembering, but I thought the girlfriend was someone with whom he'd been involved before he'd come to the island," Bessie said, trying to recall the details. "I don't know that I ever heard what happened to the man after he left the island."

"According to Todd, his father sent a bit of money for the first few years of his life and then took off to New Zealand with a third woman, leaving behind both himself and his half-sister in the UK," Jasper told her. "I gather Todd never heard from him again."

"As far as I know, he and Joney are still legally married," Bessie said. "Although I don't suppose it matters."

"Todd said something one day about his aunt discovering that his mother and father were never actually legally married," Jasper told her. "But when I asked him about it, he said I'd misunderstood what he'd said."

"That is interesting," Bessie said. "I met Todd's father only once and I've completely forgotten his name, but I do recall that I didn't care for him one bit."

"But Todd is a lovely young man," Jasper said. "He works hard, and our guests love him."

Bessie nodded. "He's waited on me more than once in your dining room. He is very good at what he does."

"So that's everyone," Andrew said. "If someone at the Seaview has been stealing credit card information, it must be one of the seven people on this list."

Jasper frowned. "I really hate to think that."

"It's an unfortunate reality," Andrew told him.

"So what do we do now?" Jasper asked.

"That depends on what you want to do," Andrew told him. "You can talk to John, and he can start a formal investigation into the thefts. You can wait and see if any additional guests ring with the same complaints. Or Bessie and I can conduct our own discreet investigation and see what we can discover."

Jasper smiled brightly and then sobered. "Are you quite certain you have time to investigate? I know you're working on another cold case."

"We can make the time," Andrew assured him. "It would probably be best if we simply started by trying to talk to all of the suspects informally. How many of them are working today?"

"Unfortunately, only Sandra is here right now. Peter and Todd will both be working dinner, though."

Andrew looked at Bessie. "Fancy having dinner here tonight?" he asked.

"I'd love to," she replied.

Andrew looked at his watch and then at Bessie. "We've several hours to fill until then."

"I'd appreciate a chance to start going through my case file," she replied.

"If you'd rather not drive all the way back to Laxey before dinner, you're more than welcome to stay here and work," Jasper told them. "Or you can move down to the library or any one of a dozen other spaces."

"I'm afraid the library would be too tempting," Bessie replied with a laugh. "I'd end up browsing the shelves instead of working."

"Stay here, then," Jasper suggested.

"Only if you take the food away," Bessie said. "If you leave it here, I'll simply keep eating, and then I won't want dinner."

Jasper nodded and then got up and crossed to the phone near the door. He picked up the receiver and pressed a button. After a few words, he put the receiver down and smiled at them. "Someone will be here momentarily to clear the room. I'll expect you in the dining room at half six if that suits you?"

"That's fine," Andrew told him. "That should give Bessie just enough time to quickly read through the bulk of the file."

Bessie opened her envelope and pulled out the contents. She studied the crime scene photo as two of Jasper's staff carefully and quietly removed the food from the table at the back of the room. As the door shut behind them, Andrew sat down next to Bessie.

"I'm going to go back through the file myself," he said as he opened his envelope. "We can talk about the case as we go."

CHAPTER 4

Bessie started at the beginning, with the report from the man who'd arrived first on the scene. Then she slowly read through Roy's statement.

"He seemed shocked and confused," she said to Andrew after she'd finished. "He kept saying that he couldn't believe what had happened and that it didn't make any sense."

Andrew nodded. "Or he could be a very good actor."

Bessie sighed. "As always, this would be easier if we could actually meet the suspects."

"Keep reading. You'll find out a lot more about all of them as you go along," Andrew suggested.

Bessie turned the page and started reading Robert's statement. "According to this, as soon as Robert arrived, he insisted on ringing the police. He says that his brother didn't have any idea what to do."

"As you said, Roy seems to have been shocked and confused."

"And Robert seems to have taken charge, even though he was the younger brother. Considering what you told us about the two brothers, I'm surprised that Robert was the one who kept calm and rang the police."

Andrew nodded. "Robert also seemed to have dealt better with being questioned by the police."

Bessie looked up from her notes. "But according to this, he'd been questioned by the police on a number of other occasions, whereas it was something completely new for Roy. Apparently, when you work as a bouncer, you spend a lot of time talking to the police."

"I have copies of the police reports from the various incidents in which Robert was involved before his parents died. I didn't bother to copy them for everyone, as they're all very similar, and I don't believe they're relevant. They were all bar fights at the club where Robert worked. From what I could determine, it was a pretty rough club."

"Robert already knew Jake from those previous incidents, then. His interview sounds a good deal more informal than Roy's had been."

"And that's down to Robert and Roy, not Jake," Andrew told her. "Robert was more relaxed about the whole thing."

"Roy insisted that his parents didn't have any reason to want to die, but Robert suggested that his father had health concerns and that his mother had often said that she didn't want to live longer than her husband."

"Something that Roy claims he never heard her say."

Bessie frowned. "One of them is lying."

"Or maybe Leo and Anna had very different conversations with Roy and with Robert. Maybe Anna and Robert were close enough for her to feel comfortable sharing her feelings with him in a way that she didn't with her older son."

"Do you think that's what happened?"

Andrew shrugged. "I have very different relationships with each of my children. I'm closest to Helen, and there are definitely things I would tell her that I wouldn't discuss with my other children. Having said that, there was no evidence that Leo was suffering from any serious health concerns in the way that Robert claimed."

"So he was lying about that much, anyway."

"Or he'd been misinformed."

"Did Jake ask Robert where he'd heard about his father's ill health?" Bessie asked.

"Not in the initial interview. At that point, Jake didn't have the autopsy report. He did ask in a follow-up interview after the autopsy, though."

"And what did Robert say?"

"That it was Leo himself who'd said he was unwell. Robert told Jake that he and his father had had something of a disagreement at the end of June. You can read it all for yourself, but, basically, Robert asked his father for a small loan and Leo refused. According to Robert, Leo told him that he was not well and that he and Anna needed every penny they had to pay for some unspecified medical treatment that Leo was going to need in the near future."

Bessie frowned and then quickly flipped through the file until she found the follow-up interview with Robert. She read it quickly and then looked up at Andrew.

"According to this, Leo wouldn't tell him anything further, and he didn't feel as if he could discuss it with his mother because he knew how she felt about being left on her own without Leo. And Roy didn't know anything about any of this?"

"Apparently not."

"Which may mean that it isn't true. Considering that the autopsy didn't reveal anything, it probably isn't true, actually, but that doesn't mean that Robert is the one who is lying," Bessie said thoughtfully.

"What do you mean?"

"I mean, maybe Leo told Robert that he was unwell for some reason, even though it wasn't true."

"Maybe he simply wanted to get Robert to stop asking him for money."

"That's one possibility. I don't suppose it's possible that Leo's doctor lied to him about some diagnosis?"

"I suppose it's possible, but, according to the medical reports, Leo hadn't seen his doctor in almost a year. He'd had an annual physical the previous September and had an appointment for another one for September again."

Bessie flipped back to where she'd been and read through Robert's statement a second time.

"He doesn't sound surprised by what happened," she said eventually. "Maybe he just seems much less surprised than his brother. Of course, he was able to offer Jake a motive for the murder-suicide pact, even if it wasn't true."

She turned the page and read through the description of the crime scene. Then she read it a second time.

"If this is a complete listing of everything found with the bodies, then there are some things missing," she said.

"Keep reading," Andrew told her.

Bessie turned the page and read the next report. "So the syringes that were used to administer the poison were in the kitchen rubbish container. According to this, Leo probably had just enough time to inject himself and then drop the syringe into the rubbish before crawling into bed next to Anna. By that time, Anna would have already been dead, of course."

"Jake told me that they counted the steps from the kitchen to the bedroom and timed exactly how long it would have taken for Leo to get from one place to the other. Robert and Roy both agreed that their father didn't walk very fast, at least not usually. Jake reckons Leo would have had to walk at an uncomfortably fast pace in order to get into bed before the poison started to have an effect on him."

"Is that one of the reasons why he doesn't believe it was a murder-suicide pact?"

Andrew nodded. "But if you keep reading, you'll find more reasons."

Bessie went back to the report. She read the next section several times before she spoke again. "There was no trace of any container that might have been used to bring the poison into the house," she said after a moment.

"There was not."

"Jake says that it's possible that Leo simply filled the syringes and carried them home, ready to use, but he also says that that seems highly unlikely."

"Syringes aren't designed to transport things from place to place, especially not deadly poisons. Leo would have had to smuggle them into the lab in the first place, then fill them, and then smuggle them back out again. It would have been far easier for him to simply pocket a small bottle of the poisonous liquid. Then he could have filled the syringes at home, at his convenience."

"But surely someone might have noticed if a bottle of poison disappeared?"

"Apparently inventory controls were not as tight as they should have been," Andrew replied. "You can read all about it yourself, but the laboratory manager admitted as much when he was interviewed. During regular working hours, they didn't even monitor access to the building. Anyone could have walked in and then wandered around the labs."

"Leo had retired some years earlier, right? Do they think he took the poison with him when he left, or went back for it later?"

"Jake and I talked about that. You'll find lots of complicated information about the poison towards the back of the file. Basically, it would have retained its potency in the proper storage bottle for at least five years, but maybe not much longer. In a syringe, it would have lost potency much more quickly, but the officials at the lab weren't certain how much more quickly."

"Did Leo ever go back and visit his former employer?" Bessie asked.

"Very regularly," Andrew told her. "There's an entire section of interviews with the man's former work colleagues."

Bessie flipped past the crime scene photos and the inventory of the contents of the house. While that was interesting, what was missing seemed much more important than what was there. She stopped when she reached a section of transcripts of interviews from Leo's former work colleagues.

"It's getting late," she said, glancing at her watch. "We need to get downstairs to the restaurant."

Andrew sighed. "Obviously, I want to do whatever we can to help Jasper, but I can't help but wish that we could keep going through the file instead of having a multi-course meal in the restaurant here."

"We don't have to have dinner here."

Andrew chuckled. "As I said, I want to do whatever we can to help Jasper. If word gets out that someone here is skimming credit cards, people might start cancelling their bookings in droves."

"Which would be a real shame," Bessie said as she slowly got to her feet.

"It would be. The Seaview is a lovely old hotel, and Jasper and Stuart work very hard to protect its reputation."

"I'm not sure what Stuart does, actually," Bessie said with a small chuckle. "I know he drives Jasper crazy, but isn't that what partners do?"

Andrew laughed. "As I understand it, Stuart bankrolled

the vast majority of the purchase of the hotel and paid for most of the needed remodelling and repair work. I think he's happy to leave Jasper to deal with the customers."

Bessie nodded. "And I'm pretty sure Jasper loves his job."

Andrew put his file back into his envelope and then put his briefcase on the table and opened it. "Do you want me to put your envelope in here, too?" he asked Bessie as he dropped his inside the case.

"Yes, please. Then I won't have to worry about it while we're having dinner." Bessie handed her file to Andrew, and he added it to the case.

"I wonder what specials the chef has prepared today," Andrew said as they made their way towards the lifts.

"I'd love to have that chicken dish again, the one we had in April or May," Bessie said.

"I still have fond memories of that one meal I had back in February," Andrew replied. "And I have very fond memories of a great many puddings."

Bessie laughed. "I hope the new pastry chef has added everything we've tried to the pudding menu."

"Oh, I hope not," Andrew countered. "I'll never be able to pick just one pudding if he has."

"I hadn't thought of that, but you're right. I hope the new pastry chef has added one or two things to the pudding menu, though. Some of the fairy cakes we were given were wonderful."

The pair chatted about food as they rode the lift to the ground floor and then slowly made their way to the restaurant. Jasper was waiting for them near the entrance.

"Dinner is my treat tonight, as you're doing me a favour," he told them in a low voice. "I've already told Peter to bill everything to my account, no arguments."

Bessie thought about disagreeing, but Jasper was clearly upset and she didn't want to make things any worse.

"What's wrong?" she asked.

Jasper sighed. "I've had another guest ring to say that his credit card was used fraudulently after his stay here. He wasn't blaming anyone here necessarily, because he had used the card all over the island, but he wanted me to know that he'd had an issue, in case the problem was here."

"I don't suppose he used the card only at reception," Andrew said.

Jasper shook his head. "He used it at reception and here in the restaurant, although only twice. Peter was here on both occasions, and he was waited on by Sherry once and Todd once."

"Does that eliminate Al from consideration?" Bessie asked.

"Maybe," Jasper said. "I'm not certain what to think, though."

"You should think about other things and let Bessie and me worry about the credit card thefts for a day or two," Andrew told him. "Obviously, let us know if you have any additional complaints, but otherwise, leave it with us."

Jasper nodded. "Thank you," he said. "I'm not very good at not worrying, but I'll try to worry a bit less, anyway."

"Please do," Bessie said, giving him a quick hug.

"And now, a table for two," Jasper said. "Right this way."

Bessie and Andrew followed Jasper across the room to a small table in the corner. "Todd will be right with you," Jasper told them as they settled into their seats.

Jasper had gone only a few paces before the young man in the black waiter's uniform rushed towards their table, menus in hand.

"Good evening," he said as he handed them each a menu. "I'm Todd, and I'll be your server this evening. Would you care to order drinks while you look at the menu?"

Bessie asked for coffee and Andrew ordered a fizzy drink.

Todd wrote their order on a notepad and then flipped through the pages.

"Let me tell you about tonight's specials before I get your drinks," he said, before launching into a long list of dishes, all of which sounded wonderful. "I'll be right back to take your order," he added at the end before he rushed away.

"We're going to get excellent service because he knows that we know Jasper," Andrew said.

"And Jasper is paying for the meal, so you can't put it on your credit card and see if the details get stolen."

"I can't imagine our thief would be so bold as to steal information from one of Jasper's friends."

"Maybe not."

"We need to find a way to start a conversation with Todd. I want to find out more about him."

"No problem," Bessie said with a grin.

The young man was back a short while later. He put their drinks on the table and then smiled at Bessie. "Are you ready to order?" he asked.

Bessie nodded and then frowned. "But how is your mother?" she asked. "Someone told me the other day that she wasn't well."

Todd frowned. "Really? Who was that, then?"

"I wish I could remember," Bessie said with a shrug. "I talk to so many people every day, and I hear so much skeet that I sometimes forget who said what."

"Yes, well, thank you for asking. Mum is fine, or at least as fine as she's ever been. She's getting older, of course, and her health has never been good, but she's still doing as well as can be expected."

"And your aunt? How is Betty? I haven't seen her in years now. I really must pay her a visit one day."

"Aunt Betty is good. She spends a lot of time with Mum

when I'm working, so that Mum doesn't get lonely," Todd told her.

"How kind of her. I'm sure your mother must appreciate her sister's efforts."

Todd made a face and then quickly nodded and smiled. "Of course she does, but it is difficult for her. She hates that she has to live with certain limitations because of her health. She doesn't complain to me very often because she doesn't want me to feel guilty, but she does complain to Aunt Betty."

"Why would you feel guilty?" Andrew asked.

Todd flushed. "I shouldn't, really, because it wasn't my fault, but my mother wasn't supposed to have children. Pregnancy was really hard on her, and it probably made her heart condition worse. She reckons she'd be able to do a lot more if she'd never fallen pregnant."

"But, as you said, that wasn't your fault at all," Bessie said firmly.

"Can I ask you something?" Todd asked after a moment.

"Of course," Bessie replied.

"Is it terribly expensive, hiring an advocate?"

"That rather depends on whom you hire," Bessie told him.

He sighed. "I want Mum to have the best, but I'm fairly certain we can't afford Doncan Quayle. He is the best on the island, though, isn't he?"

"I certainly think so. I've been using him for years, and I used his father first," Bessie said. "I hope you aren't in any trouble."

"Trouble? Oh, no, not really. It's for Mum, not me." Todd looked around the room and then stepped closer to Bessie. "It's my dad. He's been ringing lately, wanting to talk to me."

"And you don't want to talk to him?" Bessie asked.

Todd shrugged. "I don't know how I feel, but Mum doesn't want to talk to him. She doesn't want me to talk to him, either. She's afraid he's only come back to try to get his hands on her money." Todd laughed. "It isn't as if she has much, but she does own the house, and you know what house prices have done in the past few years."

Bessie nodded. While house prices had risen throughout her life, they'd skyrocketed in recent years to levels that Bessie had never imagined they'd reach.

"Anyway, Mum seems to think that she and my father weren't actually legally married, but she needs an advocate to prove it. If they weren't, then he shouldn't be entitled to anything after she dies. I just need to find an advocate that we can afford."

Bessie frowned and then pulled out her notebook and made herself a note. "Ring Doncan Quayle's office on Monday afternoon," she told Todd. "I'll speak to him first and let him know that you'll be ringing. I suspect he'll be happy to help your mother with her small matter and that he won't charge much for his services."

Todd stared at her for a moment. "Do you really think he won't charge much?"

"I'm certain of it," Bessie replied. Not only did she know that Doncan could be very generous with his time to help out people in need, but she was also prepared to pay for his services on Joney's behalf if need be.

"Thank you so much," Todd said. He shook his head and then slowly wandered away, looking dazed and confused.

"He's forgotten to take our order," Andrew said as they watched the man walk into the kitchen.

"He'll be back," Bessie said with a small laugh.

He was back only a few moments later, full of apologies. He took their order and then kept them supplied with drink refills until the food was ready.

"I'm almost getting tired of seeing Todd," Bessie murmured after the man had refilled their drinks again as they started eating.

"He's very attentive," Andrew replied. "But understandably so."

They finished their meal with items from the new pudding menu. Andrew left Todd a generous tip before the pair headed for the door.

"We didn't talk to Peter," Bessie said as they crossed the room.

"But now is our chance," Andrew replied, nodding towards the young man who was standing near the exit watching their approach.

CHAPTER 5

"Good evening," Peter said when they reached him. "I kept trying to get over to your table for a chat, but things are rather busy tonight."

"It is busy tonight," Bessie agreed as she looked back across the mostly full dining room.

"Our summer guests don't seem to want to eat anywhere else," Peter said.

"Having just had an amazing meal, I can't say that I blame them," Bessie replied with a laugh.

Peter grinned. "I'm glad you enjoyed your meal."

"And pudding," Andrew added. "Pudding was excellent."

"The new pastry chef is very talented," Peter replied. "We were lucky to get him."

"I just hope he stays forever," Bessie said.

"We're doing everything we can to keep him. I can't see him moving to a different restaurant on the island, but I do worry about him going back across."

"Oh?"

Peter shrugged. "He's only been on the island for a few months and he's still adjusting to its unique qualities. So far he's happy here, but you know as well as I do that the island isn't for everyone."

Bessie nodded. "I can't imagine living anywhere else."

"No, I can't either. I'm fortunate to have found a partner who feels the same way."

"I'd heard that you and Sandra were seeing one another."

Peter nodded. "She helped me get this job, which has been brilliant. Right after I started here, I asked her to have dinner with me, just to thank her, and, well, we've been together ever since. Mr. Coventry is helping both of us with our careers, and he doesn't seem to mind that we're together."

"Are you still in school?" Bessie asked.

"Yes, but I'm focussed on business management now. I've already learned things that have helped with the job here, and I know I'm going to learn a lot more while I work towards my degree."

"Good for you."

"And who knows, maybe in another year or two you'll need to buy a hat," he told Bessie.

She grinned at him. "I'd like that very much." It had been a while since she'd been to a wedding, and she thought that Sandra and Peter were well suited.

"I've started saving up for a ring, but I've never been very good at saving money," Peter told her. "I'm doing my best, though. Sandra is worth it."

"I suspect she'd be quite happy with something affordably priced."

Peter shrugged. "But I want to buy her the most fabulous ring I can find. I saw one in a jewellery shop window in Douglas, but it was four thousand pounds. I know Sandra would love it, but I could never afford that."

"And it would be silly to spend that much on jewellery," Bessie suggested. "You're both still in school, and you'll want to buy a house once you're married."

"I can't imagine we'll ever be able to afford a house, not with the way prices have been climbing on the island. Maybe we should look at moving across. There have to be places in England where houses are cheaper."

"I'm sure there are, but you'd miss the island," Bessie said.

Peter nodded. "I would, but I think Sandra would miss it more. She's not even from the island, but she's well and truly fallen in love with it in the time she's been here. I don't think I could do or say anything to get her to leave."

"I'm sorry to interrupt," Todd said from behind Bessie. "But the gentleman at table six wants to talk to a manager."

Peter sighed. "I knew he was going to be trouble when they arrived. He's trying to impress the woman with him by spending lots of money on dinner and complaining loudly about everything. I suspect he's hoping he can get out of paying for their very expensive meals."

"Good luck," Bessie told him.

"Thanks," Peter replied.

Bessie and Andrew watched as Peter crossed the room and began to speak to the young man at table six. After a moment, Bessie looked at Andrew.

"As we can't hear what's being said, we may as well go," she suggested.

Andrew laughed. "You're right, of course, although I am curious."

It took them only a few minutes to walk back through the hotel to the large lobby. Sandra was behind the reception desk. She smiled at them as they approached.

"You don't usually work this late," Bessie said when she reached the desk.

Sandra nodded. "Colin was supposed to be here at six, but his littlest child fell and hurt his arm, so Colin needed to stay home with the other kids while his wife took the baby to hospital."

"Oh dear. I'm not certain for whom I feel most sorry," Bessie exclaimed.

Sandra chuckled. "And people wonder why I don't want children."

"They can be incredibly hard work," Andrew said. "Obviously, I'm obliged to add that they're worth it."

Bessie and Sandra both laughed.

"How are you finding school?" Bessie asked.

"It's good. Peter and I have two classes together, so we can help each other, which is nice. And Mr. Coventry is brilliant about letting us study when it's quiet here. That isn't very often right now, because we're so busy in the summer, but I did a lot of extra studying in the spring."

"I'm glad you're happy here," Bessie said.

"And I have you to thank for it," Sandra said. "I haven't forgotten, and I'm still incredibly grateful."

"I was happy to help, and I didn't do much, anyway," Bessie replied.

"You believed in me when other people were accusing me of theft," Sandra countered. "If you hadn't been there for me through that, I would have left the island without a proper reference, and goodness only knows what would have happened to me."

"You'd have been fine," Bessie said. "You're smart and you're stronger than you think you are."

Sandra blinked back a tear. "Thank you. Coming from you, that really means a lot."

They chatted for a few additional minutes, mostly about Peter and how wonderful he was, until Andrew cleared his throat.

"We should be going," he suggested when Bessie looked at him. "It's getting late."

Bessie sighed and then nodded. "You're right. I still have a number of things I want to do tonight."

She said her goodbyes to Sandra and followed Andrew out of the building.

"I want to finish going through the file tonight," she said as Andrew drove them back towards Laxey.

"I thought you would."

"I'm already feeling frustrated with the case, though. How are we meant to determine if Leo and Anna were murdered or not? Jake is there and he has access to all of the evidence and the witnesses. If he can't work it out, I can't see how we can."

"He's hoping we'll find something that he missed when we go back through the file," Andrew told her. "At the very least, he's hoping we might narrow down his list of suspects. Or maybe we'll suggest that he look more closely at someone who didn't make his short list. He's just hoping we'll be able to suggest something that might move the case forward a little bit. He isn't expecting us to perform a miracle and solve it, though."

"I was expecting us to solve it," Bessie said. "Or rather, I always hope that we'll solve every case. This one feels more impossible than the others have, though."

"It's certainly challenging in different ways to our previous cases. But it's also interesting, and I do think we might be able to help."

"Let's see if I share your optimism after I've read the entire file."

Andrew parked in the small parking area just outside of Bessie's cottage. The cottage had been her home since she'd purchased it not long after her eighteenth birthday. In the years since, she'd added two small extensions, but it had been decades since the last addition, and she had no intention of doing anything further with her snug home. Her heirs could worry about updating Treoghe Bwaane, as the cottage was called, if they wanted to live in it after Bessie was gone.

"Widow's Cottage," Andrew said thoughtfully as he patted the sign next to Bessie's door. The sign was in Manx, but Bessie had translated it for him years earlier.

"It felt appropriate at the time," Bessie told him.

"Because the cottage already had its name when you bought it. You told me that before, but I never did ask why it was called Widow's Cottage."

Bessie stared at him for a moment and then chuckled. "You probably won't believe me, but I've no idea. When I came to see the cottage, the name was on a small sign attached to the door. Years later, when I had to have the door replaced, I had the sign that's out there now made and put up on the wall next to the new door."

"You didn't save the old sign?"

"It was badly battered and worn from years of exposure to salty sea air. I did ask the men who removed the door to save it for me, but it fell to pieces when they tried to take it off the door."

"Surely you know something about whoever owned the cottage before you bought it."

Bessie slowly shook her head. "Remember that I wasn't from Laxey, and I'd spent the sixteen years before I bought the cottage living in the US. I bought the cottage here because I wanted to get away from my parents, and this cottage felt isolated and quite distant from where they were staying in Peel. For the first few years after I moved in, I mostly kept to myself. I don't think I even spoke to my nearest neighbours for the first year or so. I was in mourning and living on my own for the first time, and I felt quite overwhelmed by everything."

"You were only eighteen."

"And I'd lived a fairly sheltered life up until that point. I really wasn't ready to live on my own, unsupervised, but that was what I chose to do."

"I wonder if you could find out anything about the cottage now," Andrew said.

Bessie frowned. "Now that you've said that, I'm going to have to try."

"But not until after we work out what happened to Leo and Anna," Andrew suggested.

"And not until after we help Jasper with the problem at the Seaview," she added. "And I have to ring Doncan and get him to agree to help Joney Hoffman, too."

"You're a very busy lady."

"Which means I'd better get back to reading my case file."

Andrew grinned and then opened his briefcase and pulled out the two envelopes from the top of the case. He gave Bessie hers and then set his on the kitchen table.

"Would you mind terribly if I make myself a cuppa?" he asked.

"Not at all. In fact, you can make me one, too," Bessie said as she sat down at the table. It wasn't like her to let someone else make tea in her kitchen, but she was so eager to get back to the case file that she didn't care. Tuning out the sounds of Andrew filling the kettle, she opened the file and found her place.

"I'm glad I've never had a neighbour like Scott Bailey," Bessie said as Andrew put her teacup next to her.

"He does come across as somewhat unpleasant."

"It's horrible, but if he's still living in the same house, I almost hope that he still hasn't received permission for his extension. I can't imagine why he'd been fighting for it for so long. Surely he could have simply bought another, larger house if that's what he wanted."

Andrew nodded. "It does seem as if he'd upset himself and everyone in the neighbourhood over the extension. I'm going to ask Jake about it, actually. At the time, Scott was living alone in a house with three bedrooms and two bathrooms. Why did he need more living space?"

"It's clear from his interview that he didn't care for Leo and Anna."

"Because they kept objecting to his plans."

"I wonder if there was more to it than that," Bessie said thoughtfully. "I'm also confused as to why they all kept up the pretense that they were friendly, when they clearly weren't."

"Maybe that's how Americans deal with their neighbours. Maybe they all hate one another but pretend to get along."

Bessie chuckled. "I have had a few somewhat unpleasant neighbours over the years, and I was always nice to them when we met on the beach or elsewhere, but that niceness didn't extend to inviting them to parties at my cottage."

"Did you have many parties at your cottage in the past?"

Now Bessie laughed. "Now that you mention it, no, I did not have many parties here. In fact, I don't think I've ever had a proper party here, not of the size and scale of the party that the Jordans had on the Fourth of July, anyway."

"And according to all accounts, they held such parties fairly regularly."

"Yes, Roy mentioned similar parties for Memorial Day and Labour Day, which are in the spring and autumn each year. He also said that they had large family gatherings at his parents' house for Thanksgiving, Christmas, and Easter every year."

"And it seems as if Scott was included in nearly all of them."

Bessie nodded. "Although he doesn't sound as if he was at all grateful for the invitations."

"He didn't seem to appreciate them, but he still went to everything to which he was invited. I'm sure he said something about spending Thanksgiving with the Jordans."

Bessie quickly skimmed through the interview she'd just read. "Yes, it's here. He says that he usually had Thanksgiving dinner with them because he didn't have any family in the area, and Thanksgiving wasn't a holiday you could spend with friends."

"Didn't he complain about some aspect of it, though?"

Bessie nodded. "He says he was always actively looking for somewhere else to go because Anna only made pumpkin pies and he preferred apple. He also complained about the quantity of leftovers he was usually given."

Andrew shook his head. "I wonder if the Jordans realised how much Scott disliked them."

"If they had, surely they would have stopped inviting him to things."

"I suspect they felt as if they had little choice. It isn't as if they could have had a party without Scott knowing about it. He was right next door."

"If I'd disliked someone as much as Scott seems to have disliked Anna and Leo, I wouldn't socialise with them. I also can't imagine fighting for such a long time over an extension."

"Does all of that make him a likely suspect in the murder investigation, though?"

Bessie frowned. "I've only read his preliminary interview. I need to read the rest of the file before I answer that."

"I'll tell you where I am, then. I've read the rest of the file, and I find it difficult to believe that Scott killed them."

"He seems like a thoroughly disagreeable person, but he doesn't seem like a killer to me," Bessie agreed. "But I reserve the right to change my mind later."

"Of course."

Bessie picked up a biscuit and nibbled on it absentmindedly while she continued reading. After half an hour, she sighed and then looked up at Andrew.

"Of all of the people involved in the case, I most want to meet Colleen."

Andrew looked surprised. "Really? Why?"

"In her interviews, she comes across as completely horrible. I want to know if she's truly that bad."

Andrew chuckled. "I have to believe that she can't have been as bad as she seems. She and Roy were together for ten years, and she remained friendly with his family after that. She must have some redeeming qualities."

"Well, they didn't come out in her interviews. In both of them, she sounds as if she's a spoiled and sulky child. Most of her answers are short and unhelpful, and she seems completely emotionally detached."

"She does come across as rather cold."

"I hope Roy was questioned at some point about their relationship. I'm curious what he would say about her."

"She didn't say much about him."

"She didn't say much about anything." Bessie flipped back through the papers in front of her. "Jake asked her about her relationship with Roy, and she said it was old news and not relevant. When he asked about her continuing friendship with Leo and Anna, she just said she had lots of friends."

"Which seems difficult to believe," Andrew murmured.

Bessie laughed. "It does seem difficult to believe, actually."

"She did say that she was shocked that Leo and Anna had chosen to end their lives in such a way. When Jake suggested that they'd both been murdered, she claimed to be even more shocked by that idea."

"She said that they were just ordinary people, and that ordinary people don't get murdered," Bessie remembered. "She seemed to think that a murder-suicide pact was more likely to have been what happened."

"I'm going to make more tea," Andrew said as Bessie turned the page in her file.

When the tea was ready, she took another break. "I don't know what to think of Russell Newton," she said after her first sip.

"In his interviews, he does seem rather enigmatic. I want Jake to ask him a lot more questions, but I'm not certain what he should ask him. I just finished reading the interview feeling as if I had missed something."

Bessie nodded. "That's exactly it. He answered all of Jake's questions, in some cases with very complex answers, but I still feel as if he was hiding something."

"Maybe something to do with where the poison came from."

"That's probably it. That could be the key to solving the entire case, but Jake never got a clear answer."

"Russell suggested very strongly that Leo had taken the poison from the lab at some point during his years working there, but when he was pushed, he insisted that as far as he knew, none of the poison had ever gone missing from the lab."

"But then he said that they didn't keep a very strict inventory of such things because people in different departments worked with different supplies all the time, and trying to track every drop of one particular chemical or another made getting work done too difficult."

"So anyone who worked in the building, from Leo to Roy to Russell, could have helped himself to a small amount of the necessary poison."

"That should mean that Roy and Russell are at the top of the suspect list," Bessie suggested.

"Unless Leo took the poison out of the lab himself. Russell did suggest that some of his colleagues have helped themselves to various supplies over the years as something of an insurance policy against suffering from a terminal illness."

Bessie shuddered. "I hate the thought of anyone committing suicide."

"But I'm sure you can understand why some people might prefer it to living with a terminal condition."

"I do understand, but did Leo? Did he really help himself to some poison just in case he fell ill in the future? And if he did take the poison himself, did he actually decide to use it that night in July? And if he did decide to use it, what made him act then? None of this makes any sense."

"And you still have pages and pages of the report to read," Andrew said. "Maybe I should leave you alone so that you can get on with it."

"As much as I hate to see you go, I do need to focus. I want to read the rest of the file before I go to bed, and I'll never manage that if we keep stopping for tea and conversation."

Andrew got up and walked towards the door. "Helen has probably already gone to bed."

"If she hasn't, tell her that I'm glad she's back on the island with you and that she's welcome to walk with me in the morning."

He nodded. "I'll let her know. I'll see you in the morning."

Andrew let himself out, leaving Bessie with her case file.

CHAPTER 6

Bessie kept reading, taking notes as she went. It was much later than her usual bedtime when she finally reached the last page of the file. She read through the interview with one of Leo's former work colleagues and then put all of the paperwork back in its envelope. Sighing, she got to her feet and stretched.

"I can see why Jake narrowed the list to those five," she said, talking quietly to herself. "But I'm not convinced that it wasn't a murder-suicide pact. According to the handwriting expert, Leo definitely wrote the note. That seems pretty conclusive."

As she talked, she wandered around the kitchen, tidying up everything that Andrew had used while making tea. Because her mind was racing, she decided to do the washing-up, hoping it would distract her from the case.

"No one had a motive for killing Leo and Anna," she said as she ran water to fill the sink. "But they didn't have any reason to end their own lives, either," she added as she slid the teacups into the hot, soapy water.

"What about means and opportunity?" she asked herself.

"That rather depends on who obtained the poison. If Leo took it himself, then who might have known about it? I can't imagine Leo telling anyone that he'd stolen some deadly poison from his former employers, but maybe Anna was less discreet."

She rinsed the last of the plates and put it in the rack next to the sink. "Opportunity is tricky, too. Someone had to come back after the party and persuade Leo and Anna to let them in. I suppose it would be easy enough for someone to claim that they'd left their phone or their handbag behind, though. All of the suspects had been guests at the party just a few hours earlier. I can't imagine that either Leo or Anna was worried about one of their guests killing them."

Shaking her head, she switched the ringer off on her telephone. That was the one concession she was willing to make to her age – although, if pressed, she'd probably insist that it was more to do with wanting a good night's sleep than worry about struggling to get down the stairs in the middle of the night. After checking that all the doors and windows were securely locked, she headed for the stairs.

"Everyone insists that they were all at home, tucked up in bed, when the Jordans died," she told her reflection as she brushed her short grey bob. "But none of the main five suspects can prove it. They all lived alone at the time. Scott lived right next door. The others would have needed to drive over to the Jordans' house, although I suppose the killer could have parked somewhere nearby rather than parking right outside."

She changed into her nightgown and then crawled under the covers. "I really do need to stop talking to myself," she muttered as she switched off the light.

BESSIE WOKE with a start just minutes after six the next morning. "How terribly unpleasant," she murmured, shaking her head to get rid of dreams that had been filled with angry men wielding syringes full of poisonous liquids.

In the kitchen, she made herself some toast and added a thick layer of honey. She washed it down with a cup of tea and told herself that she felt much better. Someone knocked on the door as she was pulling on her shoes.

"Good morning," she said brightly.

"Good morning," Helen, Andrew's daughter, replied. "My father said that I was welcome to join you on your walk this morning."

"You're always welcome to join me," Bessie assured her. "How are you?"

Helen shrugged. "I'm a bit frustrated, really," she said.

"Tell me all about it while we walk." Bessie pulled on a light jacket and then let herself out of the house. After locking the door behind herself, she set off towards the water at a brisk pace. Helen caught up as Bessie turned right at the water's edge.

"I've had to bring quite a bit of work with me this month," Helen explained. "My employers have been very understanding about my needing to be away from the office for a fortnight each month, but I'm starting to feel as if their tolerance is wearing a bit thin."

"Oh dear. What a shame."

"I was already planning on not coming with my father next month, but I may have to stay in London for the next several months. When I'm here I worry about my job, but when I'm there, I'm going to worry about my father."

"Can someone else come with him?" Bessie asked. "He told me that his doctors don't want him travelling on his own."

"They don't, and yes, of course, someone else will come

with him. My brother is coming next month. That's already all arranged. I should probably apologise for him now, before you even meet him."

Bessie raised an eyebrow. "Is he that bad?"

Helen sighed. "He's not a bad person. I'm probably being unfair. He's going through a very difficult divorce, though, one that just keeps getting worse and worse. His former wife seems ready to lie, cheat, and steal her way into getting every penny she can from him, and he's more than a little bitter and angry."

"I am sorry."

"It doesn't help that I never cared for her. She was Matt's second wife. His first wife was lovely and sweet and wonderful, but they drifted apart over the years. Eventually, they divorced amicably, mostly for the sake of the children. Matt swore he was never going to get married again, and then he met Abigail." Helen sighed.

"I don't know that I've ever heard someone express so much dislike for another person in just saying his or her name," Bessie said.

Helen frowned. "I tried to like her. When they first got together, I took her out for lunch a few times and did my best to get to know her. She wasn't at all interested. After a few weeks, I stopped trying."

"And now they're getting divorced."

"I'm surprised it took this long, really. But yes, they're getting divorced, and it's taking ages to work its way through the courts, and every delay costs Matt even more money. Right now, I'm pretty sure he'd pay just about anything to get rid of Abigail for good, but apparently no amount of money will speed up the process, not while Abigail is dragging her feet, anyway."

"So now your brother is going to come to the island with your father."

"Matt needs to get away from London and Abigail and, well, everything, really. The change of scenery will be good for him, and I think he'll enjoy spending some time with Dad, too. They haven't done anything together, just the two of them, in years."

"How is your father?" Bessie asked.

Helen laughed. "You've spent more time with him in the past twenty-four hours than I have. I should be asking you that question."

"He seems perfectly fine to me. If I didn't know better, I'd never suspect that there is anything wrong with him."

Helen nodded. "He seems perfectly fine most of the time. We had some encouraging news from the doctor last week as well. While Dad is still going to need surgery some time fairly soon, the doctor was happy that his condition doesn't seem to be getting any worse. He's stable, which is surprising, given everything that's wrong with him."

"That's good to hear."

"Dad's doctor had originally said that Dad would need surgery within six months, but he's now pushed that back to twelve months, assuming Dad continues to eat right and look after himself."

"That's wonderful news."

Helen nodded. "And Dad would probably never tell you himself, because he hates talking about his health."

The pair walked in silence for a few minutes before Helen spoke again.

"I know you can't talk about the case you're considering this month, but I hope it's going well."

"It's a very frustrating one, actually. I don't think we're going to be able to help this time."

"That would be a shame, but it's hardly surprising. Dad said that he didn't expect you to be able to solve more than one or two cases in a year, and, so far, you've solved every case you've considered."

"I know, but now I'm quite spoiled and I want to keep solving them all," Bessie said with a laugh.

"I can understand that. It must be very satisfying, working out what happened years ago and putting a killer behind bars."

"It is, and I'm grateful that I've been given a chance to be a part of the unit, really. That isn't to say that it isn't very frustrating sometimes."

Helen nodded. "When I was a child, my father often talked about the frustrations of the work that he did. He loved his job, and he loved making a difference in the world, but there were times when he talked about quitting and doing just about anything else. When I was trying to decide what I wanted to do with my life, I briefly considering going into the police, but I didn't think I could deal with so many of the difficult aspects of the job."

"I know I'm struggling, and I'm on only the very fringes of actual police work," Bessie said. "And we've walked a very long way and we probably should turn around."

Helen chuckled. "We have walked rather a long way, but it's a beautiful morning for a long stroll."

They turned around and headed back towards the holiday cottages, the last of which was only just visible in the distance.

"I was afraid the beach would be full of screaming children in July," Helen said. "Yesterday there were only three children on the beach, and they were all almost weirdly quiet."

"It used to get very busy in the summer months. Everyone in Laxey seemed to come to the beach nearly every day. Once foreign holidays became so much more affordable, though, people started travelling to sunnier climates to sit on beaches there. Now it gets busy on Laxey Beach only when the holiday cottages are fully occupied by large families."

"There don't seem to be many families here at the moment."

Bessie laughed. "With you and your father in one cottage and Charles and Harry taking up two more, that doesn't leave all that many cottages for large families."

"Is Pat still living in the last cottage? I told him that I wouldn't want to live in a cottage where people had been murdered, but he doesn't seem to mind."

"I believe he's just grateful to have a roof over his head. Maggie and Thomas have been very good to him, and he's proven himself to be a hard worker, too. Maggie offered him his choice of cottages, and he decided that he'd prefer to stay in the last one. Maggie and Thomas aren't using it otherwise, as they don't want to chase away any guests who might find out about the murders after they'd already arrived on the island."

"I suppose that makes sense."

"Maggie's done her best to make the cottage feel as if it's home for Pat, anyway. It has the nicest furniture of any cottage in the row."

Helen laughed. "That isn't saying much. I love the location of the cottages, but the furniture is quite awful. It's a good thing the sea air and all these long beach walks wear me out. Otherwise, I don't think I'd ever sleep on the uncomfortable mattress in my bedroom. And I won't even mention the pillow."

"I have a spare bedroom, if you want a change of scenery," Bessie offered. "And I also have a huge pile of extra pillows, if you want to borrow a nicer one for your stay."

"I don't want to leave my father alone overnight. Otherwise, I might take you up on your first offer. As for the second, are you sure you can spare one?"

"I can spare several. Not only have I bought more for myself than I'll ever need, but I've also bought more for the spare bedroom than will ever be used. Some of them have never been out of their packaging. You're more than welcome to come back to my cottage and select a favourite."

Helen sighed. "I hate to take advantage of your generosity, but the pillows that are in the cottage are quite awful. I'm afraid I'm rather spoiled, but I do prefer feather pillows, and the ones I have in my bedroom here are most definitely not filled with feathers."

"Every pillow I own is feather and down. Come and find one that you like. I'll store it for you between visits, and you're more than welcome to use it every time you come over."

Half an hour later, Helen had tried several pillows and found one that she loved. "I still feel a bit guilty about borrowing it, but I also wish I'd complained to you sooner," she said with a laugh as she headed for the door with her pillow in her arms. "Don't be surprised if my father comes knocking in a little while, begging for a pillow, too."

"As you've just seen, I have plenty to spare. Your father would be more than welcome to one, although he's never complained about not being able to sleep here."

"He does seem to sleep here much better than he does at home. Perhaps he should trade his comfortable mattress and feather pillow in London for something a good deal less comfortable."

Bessie laughed. "I believe the sea air should get some of the credit if he is sleeping better here."

Helen nodded. "He's also simply happier here. He cares a lot about you, and he loves the work that he's doing here. Back in London, he's mostly retired and he's, well, he's rather lonely."

Bessie felt herself blushing. "I enjoy his company, too," she said, feeling awkward.

"And now I should go and see if he's out of bed yet. I need to ring my office and try to take part in a meeting at nine."

Bessie watched from the doorway as the woman walked back to her cottage, still clutching her borrowed pillow. As Helen went inside, Bessie shut the door and then locked it. She was reading through the case file a second time when someone knocked, more than an hour later.

"Hello, good morning. What's this I hear about borrowing pillows?" Andrew asked when Bessie opened the door.

She laughed. "Helen was complaining about the pillows on her bed, so I lent her a nicer pillow. You're welcome to borrow one, too."

Andrew shook his head. "I already sleep far too much when I'm here. If the bed were actually comfortable, I'd never get anything done. As it is, I've just had breakfast and it's nearly time for lunch."

Bessie glanced at the clock and shrugged. "Not quite, but you've already read the case file. I've just been going through it again."

"I hope you've come up with some good questions for Jake. I really want to solve this case for him."

"I have a few questions, but they may all be answered when we find out what everyone has been doing since the murders."

"Do you want more time with the case file, or should we find something more pleasant to do with what is left of our morning?"

Bessie thought for a moment. "I really should spend more time with the case file, but I'd rather not. I'd much rather go into Ramsey and do some window shopping."

Andrew grinned at her. "At the bookshop or elsewhere?"

"Elsewhere for window shopping, but proper shopping at the bookshop."

"Perfect."

Ten minutes later, they were on their way. Andrew found a parking spot right outside of the large bookshop that was one of Bessie's favourite places in the world. They spent a half hour browsing the shelves before Bessie paid for the five books she'd found. Andrew purchased only two books before they meandered up and down the main shopping street, looking in windows and visiting a few shops.

"Shall we have lunch at the Seaview?" Andrew asked as they walked back towards his hire car.

"Let's. Maybe we'll be able to speak to a few more of the, um, suspects in the credit card thefts."

"I'm not sure we'll manage that, but at least we'll have a nice lunch."

When they arrived at the Seaview, Bessie was surprised to find a man she'd not met before behind the reception desk.

"But where's Sandra?" she asked as she and Andrew approached the desk.

The man smiled and shook his head. "She covered for me last night because I had a small family emergency, so I took the first half of her shift today," he explained.

"You must be Colin," Bessie said. "Sandra told us that your littlest one hurt his arm."

Colin nodded. "He's going to worry my wife into an early grave, that one. We thought our first two kids were hard work, but the little one has made us realise how easy we had it with the other two. If he's not getting into trouble, he's busy thinking up his next troublemaking scheme. He's only two, and he's already been more work than the other two kids put together."

"My goodness," Bessie said.

Andrew just laughed. "Our third was difficult, too. He still is, if I'm honest, although he's considerably older than two now."

"Maybe it's something to do with being the third child," Colin said.

"Or maybe it's something to do with being the last child," Andrew suggested. "My wife did spoil our youngest a bit after we agreed that we weren't going to have any more."

Colin sighed. "My wife still wants another one, even though our third is such hard work. I keep telling her that she's going to have to go back to work soon, just so we can afford the three we have, but she really wants to stay at home until they're all in school. We might just manage it, assuming we stop at three."

"Good luck to you," Andrew said. "It's a difficult decision to make."

"But what can I help you with?" Colin asked.

"Not a thing," Bessie told him. "We're here to have lunch before our meeting at two. I suppose you could tell us where we're meeting today."

Colin nodded. "Mr. Coventry has your meeting scheduled for the conference room on the fifth floor today. Do you need directions?"

"We'll find it," Andrew told him. "Thank you."

The pair turned and walked through the lobby to the corridor that led to the dining room.

"Now we just need Al or Sherry to be working in the restaurant," Bessie whispered as they went.

"I'd prefer Sherry, as Jasper seemed to think that Al was probably no longer a suspect after his last complaint."

"And Al usually only works breakfast, so Sherry is more likely. Having said that, there must be at least four or five others who might be working."

They reached the dining room and were quickly seated at a table near the door.

"Al will be right with you," they were told.

"Al?" Bessie repeated.

"Is that a problem?" the host asked. "I can move you to another table if you'd prefer a different waiter or waitress."

"It's not a problem," Bessie said quickly. "I just thought that Al only worked in the mornings."

The man gave her a strange look and then nodded slowly. "He does usually work breakfast, but he's taking an extra shift today."

"Great," Bessie said. "Thanks." She picked up her menu and hid behind it. *And this is why I'd never make it as a spy,* she thought as Andrew chuckled softly.

CHAPTER 7

"Good morning," the man who approached the table a few minutes later said, smiling at Bessie. "I'm Al, and I'll be taking care of you this morning. Except it's technically no longer morning. I usually work breakfast, so I'm rather confused."

"Good afternoon," Bessie told him. "I do hope you know what lunch specials are available."

"I do," Al replied. He flipped through the small order book in his hand. When he found the right page, he stopped and read out a short list of specials.

"They all sound good," Bessie said with a sigh.

Al nodded. "They all taste good, too. The chef gave me a bite of each to try so that I could properly explain them to our guests. I told him I might have to switch to working lunch every day."

Bessie laughed. "I'm certain I'd gain a great deal of weight if I worked here."

"Do you know what you want, or should I get you some drinks while you look at the menu?"

"I think I need a minute," Bessie told him.

He nodded and then wrote down their drink order. "I'll be right back," he promised before he walked away.

"He seems nice enough," Bessie said when she was certain he was out of earshot.

"He does, but gambling can be a real problem for some people. He would be at the top of my list if he had waited on all four people."

"As it is, he only took care of three of them, which suggests he isn't behind the problem."

When Al came back, they both ordered.

"Any suggestions on the best place to watch the football later?" Andrew asked Al.

He shrugged. "It will be on in the bar here, for sure, and probably in every pub on the island as well. You should be able to watch it just about anywhere."

Andrew nodded. "And if it goes my way, we'll be back for dinner tomorrow night."

Al laughed. "Placed a bit of a wager on the game, have you?"

"Just a small one. I don't like to take too many risks with my hard-earned money."

"That's why I have a second job," Al told him. "My pensions pay for my daily expenses, and this job here pays for my gambling. When I take extra shifts, I can wager a bit more."

"There's an idea. Maybe I need a second job," Andrew said.

"You just have to be really strict with yourself and not spend more than you can afford," Al told him.

"Is that the voice of experience?" Andrew asked.

Al made a face. "I may have, um, overdone it a few times in the past, but I've been doing a lot better lately. I'm going to win big tonight, though, and then I'll treat myself to something special."

"What are you planning to buy?" Bessie asked.

"I'm thinking about going across to one of the tracks where they have live horse racing. If I hit big tonight, I could make a weekend out of it, stay in a nice hotel, have some fancy meals, and do a bit of wagering on the horses."

Bessie tuned the men out as they discussed racetracks and betting on horses, subjects in which she had no interest. After a few minutes, Al glanced at the clock on the wall.

"I'd better get back to work," he said. "My shift will be over, and you won't even have your food yet."

As he rushed away, Bessie looked at Andrew. "Did you get anything useful out of that?"

"I don't think so. He knows a lot about horses and gambling, but I was expecting that. He isn't going to admit to a stranger that he's deeply in debt, of course."

Bessie sighed. "I don't think we're going to be able to help Jasper at all, not unless we start asking everyone some difficult questions."

Andrew nodded. "It may come to that. For now, I'm just happy to have a chance to chat with each of the suspects."

"Do you truly think you'll be able to work out who is behind the thefts through casual conversation?"

"Not at all, but I do think I might be able to narrow down the list of suspects. Or rather, I hoped I might, but now I'm not so sure."

Al was back with their lunches a short while later. "Do you need anything else?" he asked after he'd put their plates on the table.

Bessie shook her head. "It all looks wonderful."

"Good. My shift is technically over now. If you don't mind, I'm going to turn you over to Sherry. If you need anything, just let her know," Al said.

"That's fine," Andrew replied. "I doubt we'll need anything other than the bill."

THE JORDAN FILE

Al nodded. "Sherry will have that for you whenever you're ready. Enjoy your lunch."

The pair were talking about shoes when Sherry checked on them several minutes later.

"Is everything okay?" she asked. "Can I get anyone anything?"

Bessie started to nod and then shook her head. "Everything is fine, and I don't think we need anything," she explained, laughing at herself.

"Just shout if you need anything," Sherry told her.

"We will, but how is your mother?" Bessie asked.

Sherry looked surprised. "Mum's fine."

"Tell her Bessie Cubbon was asking about her. I knew her years ago, when she was growing up in Laxey."

Sherry nodded. "I'll tell her."

"She's still in Ramsey, isn't she?" Bessie asked.

"Yeah, but maybe not for much longer."

"Oh?"

"We've been talking about moving across. My sister, Susan, is near Oxford, and we've been talking about going over and staying with her for a while. She just had a baby and she's completely overwhelmed."

"I can't imagine," Bessie said.

Sherry shrugged. "I can't, either. It's just a baby. How much time and energy can something that small need? But Mum's keen to go over and help and I'm, well, I'm not sure what I want to do, but I think I'd enjoy a change of scenery. Nothing has been decided, but we're going to have to make a decision soon."

"Well, good luck to you, whatever you choose," Bessie said.

"Thanks," Sherry replied before she strolled away.

Bessie and Andrew finished the last of their lunches.

"No pudding, thanks," Bessie told Sherry as she cleared

their plates. "We're here for a meeting and we'll have biscuits at the very least."

"Is that the meeting on the fifth floor?" Sherry asked. "When I was in the kitchen a few minutes ago, the new pastry chef was putting together a huge plate of miniature doughnuts for that meeting."

"I hope it's ours," Bessie said, suddenly wishing she'd eaten a smaller lunch.

"The doughnuts are really good," Sherry told her. "I sneaked a few off the plate when the chef wasn't looking."

Bessie frowned. That sort of behaviour seemed the sort that might make Sherry lose her job, but she could certainly sympathise with the woman's desire to try a doughnut or two.

"I'm kidding," Sherry said quickly. "The chef put out a separate plate for all of us so that we could try them, too. They're something new that he's thinking of adding to the menu."

"They sound delicious," Andrew said.

"They definitely are."

Andrew paid the bill and then the pair took the lifts to the fifth floor. Jasper was standing in the doorway to the conference room as they approached.

"Good afternoon," he said brightly.

"Good afternoon," Bessie replied.

"It's been good so far, in that I haven't had another complaint yet today," Jasper told them. "I do find myself cringing every time my phone rings, though."

"We've spoken to just about everyone," Bessie replied. "So far they all seem lovely and trustworthy."

"But they all seem to need money," Andrew said. "Maybe we can sit down and talk about them all again after our meeting."

Jasper nodded. "I'll be in my office all afternoon, hoping

the phone remains silent. You can find me there when your meeting is over."

"We will," Bessie told him. "But what is this I hear about doughnuts?"

Jasper laughed. "Everyone in the kitchen and restaurant has been talking about them all day. You have an entire plate of different ones. I want to hear your thoughts later."

Bessie nodded as she looked past Jasper at the table of food near the door. She could just see the plate that was stacked high with the tiny, tempting morsels.

"I need to go and ring back a guest who wants to bring his pet parakeet with him," Jasper said.

"Are you going to let him?" Andrew asked.

"I haven't decided yet," Jasper replied with a laugh before he walked away.

Bessie filled a plate with tiny doughnuts and poured herself a cup of coffee. Andrew did the same and then they sat together at the table, waiting for the others.

"Knock, knock," a loud voice said from the doorway.

Bessie frowned as Dan Ross stuck his head into the room.

"I was just passing through, and I had a few extra questions for you," he told Andrew. "Are there doughnuts?"

As Dan stacked more doughnuts than Bessie could count on to a plate, she glared at his back. He poured coffee into a cup and then walked over and sat down next to Andrew.

"Right, so I have my notes from yesterday. How did your meeting go after I left?"

"It was fine," Andrew replied.

"And how is the case this month? Is it murder? Do you think you'll solve it? Where did it happen? What else can you tell me?"

Andrew frowned at the long list of questions. "Fine, no comment, no comment, no comment, nothing," he said when Dan paused to shove a doughnut into his mouth.

"Yeah, right, okay," Dan said around his mouthful. "But, seriously, you need to give me more for my story. At least tell me if you're working on a murder investigation this time or not."

"I can't tell you anything about the case," Andrew replied. "Everything we do is confidential."

Dan sighed. "That isn't going to make for a very interesting story. Hey, everybody, the island has its very own cold case unit, but I can't tell you anything about the cases they investigate or their success rate. It's not really worth my time to write that article."

"Then don't bother," Bessie suggested.

Dan frowned. "The existence of the unit is news," he conceded. "I just know I could write a much more interesting article, one that would get the entire island talking, if I could have just a little bit more information."

Andrew shook his head. "I can't share anything with you, I'm afraid."

"In that case, I'll just have to speculate," Dan said. "I would imagine, since you need to keep everything a secret, that you must be investigating only the most serious of crimes. You won't be interested in little things like insurance fraud or even kidnapping. You must be only bothering with murder investigations."

"Actually, not all of our cases have been murder investigations," Andrew told him.

"Now we're getting somewhere," Dan muttered. "What else could be considered as serious as murder, though? You did mention missing persons before. What about people smuggling or drug dealing?"

Andrew picked up a doughnut and took a bite. He chewed slowly and then took a sip of his coffee. "The weather has been quite pleasant since I've been here this visit," he said eventually.

THE JORDAN FILE

Dan frowned. "Yeah, great, whatever. Bessie, just how awful are the crime scene photos in a murder investigation?"

Bessie stared at him. "I'm sure you can imagine the answer to that," she said after a long pause.

"But I've never actually seen a crime scene photo. How does it feel to see pictures of something awful that happened to some poor person you didn't know?"

"The island is usually quite nice in July," Bessie told Andrew.

Dan groaned. "Come on, just give me something I can work with. Something that will make the story interesting to the average man or woman on the island. Anything."

Andrew shook his head. "We're getting ready for our meeting now. I'm afraid I'm going to have to ask you to leave."

"At least let me finish my snack," Dan protested, shoving another treat into his mouth.

The door opened and Harry walked into the room. "I didn't realise that we were doing more interviews today," he said as he walked to the table and poured himself some coffee.

"We aren't," Andrew said. "Mr. Ross was just leaving."

Harry smiled coldly. "That's good news," he said, walking over and standing next to Dan. "Bye," he said flatly.

Dan looked up and then jumped to his feet. "Yeah, um, thanks, er, I'll, that is, um, yeah," he stammered before he rushed out the door, carrying his plate of doughnuts with him.

"I think he's afraid of you," Bessie said as Harry moved to take a seat with his back to the wall.

"He should be," Harry replied.

Bessie swallowed a dozen different replies. While she respected Harry a great deal, there was a little part of her that was just the smallest bit afraid of him as well.

81

Charles walked in a moment later. He stopped in the doorway and looked around the room. "I'm never early," he said, looking at the clock.

"The others appear to be running late," Andrew replied. "Get some doughnuts and a drink and join us."

They were talking about British politics when Doona, John, and Hugh finally arrived about ten minutes later.

"There was a large crash on the road between here and Laxey," John explained as they all filled plates. "The police already had things under control, but we had to wait for several minutes for them to clear the road and let the ambulances through."

"I hope no one was seriously hurt," Bessie said.

"Three people were taken to hospital, but none had life-threatening injuries," John replied.

"That's good news," Bessie said.

When they were all sitting together around the table, Andrew began.

"So, what did you all think of the case?" he asked.

"It's an odd one," Doona said. "I don't know what to think. At times I thought it probably was murder-suicide, but at other times I felt certain that someone killed both Anna and Leo."

"I think the missing poison bottle makes murder-suicide unlikely," Harry said. "I could just about believe that Leo put the syringes in the rubbish before he crawled into bed to die, but that doesn't explain what happened to the bottle that held the poison in the first place."

"Do we know what sort of bottle it was?" Charles asked.

Andrew frowned. "I can have Jake ask Russell or Roy how the poison was typically stored," he said.

"I think it might be useful to know," Charles said. "I assume they weren't storing it in syringes."

"According to some of his former work colleagues, Leo

visited the lab fairly regularly after his retirement. The poison was supposed to have been kept in a locked cupboard, but everyone agreed that the cupboard was occasionally left unlocked. Roy and Russell both stated that Leo might have been alone in the lab for long enough to open the cupboard, find and take a bottle of the poison, and shut the cupboard again before anyone disturbed him," Bessie said. "But they both also said that they thought it was highly unlikely that Leo would have done such a thing."

"Which is odd, because saying that puts them both at the top of the list of suspects," Hugh said. "If Leo didn't get the poison himself, then either Roy or Russell must have taken it."

"Are the police quite certain that the poison came from that particular lab?" Bessie asked.

Andrew frowned. "I can double-check, but where else could it have come from?"

"That's what I'm wondering," Bessie said. "Is it possible that it came from somewhere else? I read the reports that said that it was a very specific mixture used by that lab in a variety of different ways. Do any other labs use it for any similar purposes? And did any of our suspects have access to any of those other labs?"

"I'll send that question to Jake later today," Andrew told her. "What else?"

"Where did the syringes come from?" John asked. "Were they readily available in the lab where Leo had worked or not?"

"I'm not sure. I don't remember reading anything about that in the file," Andrew said, making a note.

"The biggest problem for me was the lack of motive," Doona said. "Leo and Anna didn't appear to have had any reason to end their lives, but it also didn't seem as if anyone else had any reason to want them dead."

"Their sons inherited a lot of money," Charles said.

"Yes, but Roy seems to have been doing fine on his own. I suppose Robert had the strongest motive, especially if his father truly was going to cut him off," Doona replied.

"Scott's claim about what he overheard didn't seem terribly credible to me," John said. "He admitted that he'd been drinking considerably and that he was quite far away from Leo and Robert when they were talking."

"It almost felt to me as if he was trying to cause trouble for Robert, although I'm not certain why," Bessie said.

Andrew nodded. "I felt the same way."

"Maybe he killed Leo and Anna and was hoping to frame Robert for the murder," Charles suggested.

"That's one possibility," Andrew replied.

"Roy did say that he couldn't imagine his father ever cutting off Robert," Bessie remembered. "Or rather, Roy said that he couldn't imagine his mother ever letting his father stop supporting Robert."

"And Robert said much the same, that his mother was always going to make sure that he was okay," Doona said.

"So we're back to no one having a motive," Hugh said with a sigh.

"Maybe Scott did kill them," Bessie said. "Maybe he was tired of fighting over his extension, or maybe there was something else going on about which we know nothing."

"Maybe Scott was running a drug-smuggling ring out of his garage and Leo found out," Hugh said.

"That seems unlikely, but there may have been other difficulties between the neighbours besides the extension. Maybe some of the other neighbours, ones who weren't even questioned during the initial investigation, might know more," Andrew said thoughtfully.

"And maybe we could find out why he didn't simply move," Bessie said. "We talked about that before."

Andrew nodded and then made himself a note.

"I couldn't imagine why Colleen would have killed them until I read her interview. She came across as very unpleasant," Doona said.

"I thought the same, but being unpleasant isn't really a motive for murder," Bessie said.

"I wonder if she wanted to try again with Roy and thought his parents were standing in her way," Hugh said. "She said something about them always saying how much better they liked her since she and Roy ended things."

"Which is just odd," Doona muttered.

"Don't you get along better now with your former mother-in-law than you did when you were married?" Bessie asked.

Doona sighed. "Yes, okay, now that you mention it, yes." She looked at the others and flushed. "I got married far too young to my very first serious boyfriend. His mother and I didn't get along very well. Looking back, it's clear that she knew that we weren't properly in love, not enough to work our way through a lifetime together, but at the time I thought she was just angry with me for taking away her little boy. After the dust settled on the divorce, I came to appreciate her a lot more, and I would go so far as to say that we're actually friends now. We get together very occasionally for coffee or lunch, and we really enjoy each other's company."

"It might be quite telling if Colleen and Roy got back together after Leo and Anna died," Bessie said. "You are going to tell us where everyone is now, aren't you?" she asked Andrew.

CHAPTER 8

Andrew chuckled. "Jake has been meeting with each of the suspects every year for the past five years. I have copies of all of those interviews for you to go through, but I'll summarise the highlights before I give them out. Before I do that, does anyone have any other questions for Jake at this point?"

"I have a few, but some of them may be answered by the updates you're about to provide," John said.

Harry nodded. "Let's hear the updates."

Andrew opened his notebook and turned a few pages. "As I said, this is just a brief summary of five years' worth of interviews. Mostly, I'm just going to tell you where everyone is now."

"Has Jake been interviewing everyone involved in the case every year or just his top five suspects?" Bessie asked.

"His top five have been interviewed every year," Andrew told her. "But he's also spoken to some of the other witnesses again, at least once or twice. In your envelope you'll find copies of every interview he's done with regard to this case."

Bessie nodded.

"Does everyone agree with Jake's top five?" Andrew asked. "There were several other people at the party the day before the bodies were found, and both Anna and Leo had other friends and even other family members. Did anyone feel as if Jake should have spent more time looking into anyone else?"

Harry sighed. "It's tricky, because he's there and he's able to see people's expressions and body language and we aren't. I certainly felt as if all five of the people he chose were likely suspects, but there were a few others that also raised my suspicions."

He read off a short list of names from his notebook. Andrew wrote them all down.

"Anyone else?" Andrew asked.

"I only had two others on my list," John said. "And Harry named them both."

"I had the same list as Harry, but with one more," Charles told him. He gave Andrew the name and Andrew added it to his list.

"I was quite happy with the five that Jake named," Doona said. "No one else seemed to have had a motive, but then neither did those five people."

"I didn't make a list," Hugh said, sounding sheepish. "No one jumped out at me, though, not any more than the five that Jake suspects."

Bessie nodded. "Without a clear motive for anyone, it's difficult to pick and choose suspects. I can see why Jake selected the five he did, but, if I'd been in his place, I don't know that I would have chosen the same five."

"Whom would you have chosen?" Andrew asked.

"I wish I knew. I think, in his place, I might have just closed the case as murder-suicide," she admitted. "He had a written confession, after all."

Andrew nodded. "And how would you have explained the missing bottle?"

"Maybe Leo filled the syringes in the garden or the garage and then brought them into the house. I'm sure both areas were searched, but maybe something was missed," Bessie replied.

"And now, updates," Charles said firmly before Andrew could reply.

Everyone laughed.

"Yes, of course," Andrew said. "Where should I start?"

"Roy," Bessie suggested.

"What do you think has happened to him?" Andrew asked.

"Did he inherit enough to quit working? Maybe he married Colleen and had a child or two," Bessie suggested.

"I can't see him marrying Colleen," Doona said. "If they didn't get married after ten years together, they weren't ever going to get married."

"Unless what happened to his parents served as a sort of catalyst and got him to propose," Charles said. "Honestly, though, I think he's still single and still working in the same lab."

"And you're right," Andrew told him. "According to him, Colleen still rings him up from time to time to see if he's interested in trying again, but he always refuses to even consider the idea."

"That makes it seem as if she was simply staying friendly with Roy's parents so that she'd have an excuse to see him," Doona said thoughtfully.

"For what it's worth, Colleen just laughed when Jake asked her about Roy and her attempts to reconcile with him. She told him that when she gets drunk and lonely, she rings every name in her address book, but that she doesn't really want to get back with Roy or with anyone else from her past," Andrew told them.

"So she's still single," Bessie said.

"She is. I'll just finish with Roy by telling you that he's been using his inheritance to travel. He still has the same job, but he takes off at every opportunity and travels the world. He hasn't been to the Isle of Man yet, but he's been a great many other places."

"How nice for him," Bessie murmured.

"Meanwhile, Colleen is, presumably, stuck in Wyoming," Charles said.

Andrew nodded. "She admitted, in a recent interview, that she had been surprised and was still disappointed that Leo and Anna hadn't left her anything. She told Jake that Leo had once told her that they would be leaving her a few little mementos to remember them by."

"Why would they leave their son's former girlfriend anything?" Doona asked.

"According to Colleen, Leo hinted that they were going to leave all of Anna's jewellery to her because neither of their sons was married. She says she always assumed that they'd change their wills if Roy or Robert ever got married, but as long as they stayed single, the jewellery would be hers," Andrew explained.

"Was there much jewellery?" Bessie asked.

"I believe there was an inventory with the wills," Andrew said.

Bessie flipped through her file and then stopped and frowned at the page in front of her. "That's quite a lot of jewellery," she said.

"Gold watches, diamond rings, gemstone bracelets, solid gold chains," Doona read down the list. "Colleen could have taken quite a lot of very nice holidays if she'd inherited all of that and then sold it."

"But there wasn't any provision in the wills for her at all," Bessie said as she looked back through the documents. "And neither Leo nor Anna had made any changes to their wills in over five years."

"So either Leo was lying to Colleen or she completely misunderstood him," Hugh said.

"Why would he lie about that?" Bessie asked.

"Colleen said she thought that Leo told her that in an effort to get her to stay away from Roy," Andrew told her. "She said that Leo hinted that they might change their minds if she and Roy got back together."

"But that doesn't even make sense," Bessie protested. "They were leaving her the jewellery because neither of their sons were married. If Roy married Colleen, then surely they would have wanted to leave her the jewellery even more."

Charles shrugged. "Roy is happily single and travelling, and Colleen is unhappily single and still disappointed in her lack of inheritance. What about Robert?" Charles asked.

"Any guesses?" Andrew wondered.

"Still single. I'd love to think that he went back to school and is now a very successful and productive member of society, but I don't think that's what happened," Harry said.

Andrew nodded. "He did not go back to school. What he did was burn through his inheritance at an alarming rate. He now lives alone, aside from his dog, in a small house, the third that he's owned since his parents died. Apparently he struggles to make ends meet, and Roy refuses to help."

"Let me guess – he bought himself a huge mansion right after his parents died," Doona said.

"He did," Andrew agreed. "Over four thousand square feet of luxurious living space, according to Jake. He lived there for a year before he sold it and moved into a smaller home. He was in that house for just about two years before he moved into the property he now owns."

"And he's remained single," Harry said.

"Yes, although in his most recent interview he did tell Jake that he and Colleen were involved briefly a few years ago," Andrew said.

"He and Colleen?" Bessie repeated. "What did Roy have to say about that?"

"It never came up in Jake's interviews with Roy," Andrew replied.

"Maybe it should have," Bessie said. "Or maybe not, as I can't actually imagine how it could be relevant to the murders. I'm just incredibly curious what Roy thought about his younger brother becoming involved with his former girlfriend."

"I can have Jake ask Roy about it," Andrew offered. "I can have him ask Colleen, too, as it never came up in the interviews with her, either."

"Maybe it never really happened," Doona suggested. "Maybe they had dinner together once or twice, and Robert thought it was the start of a relationship while Colleen thought she was just having dinner with a friend."

"Also possible," Andrew said. "Should I have Jake find out more or not?"

"Let's see what else comes up," Bessie said.

Andrew nodded. "Anyone want to speculate on where Scott is now?"

"He must still be in the same house," Doona said. "If he was prepared to live there for all those years, fighting for planning permission, then surely he hasn't moved now."

"He has not moved, and he still hasn't been able to add his extension," Andrew told them. "Apparently, once Leo and Anna passed away, the neighbours on the other side of Scott's home started objecting every time he submitted plans. In his last interview, he told Jake that he's just about ready to put his house on the market and try to find something else in, as he put it, a friendlier neighbourhood."

"Of everyone we've considered, he surely had the best opportunity to commit the murders," Bessie said thoughtfully. "He was right next door."

"That's assuming that Leo was the one who had obtained the poison," Harry said.

"Unless the poison came from somewhere other than the lab where Leo worked," Bessie countered.

Andrew looked up from his notes. "I'm going to ask Jake about that possibility. It's an intriguing one."

"That just leaves Russell," Hugh said. "Where is he now?"

"Guesses?" Andrew asked.

"He must be retired by now. Didn't you say he was in his sixties when the Jordans died?" Bessie checked.

"He was sixty-five then, which would make him seventy now, but he is still working, albeit only part-time."

"He must love his job," Doona said.

"His later interviews are quite sad, actually," Andrew told them. "Each time Jake asks him why he hasn't retired, he tells Jake that he's still working because he simply doesn't know what else to do with himself."

"That is sad," Bessie murmured.

"Did Jake ever actually ask him if he'd had an affair with Anna?" Harry asked. "Someone hinted that there was something there. In his initial interview, Russell just said that he was friendly with both Leo and Anna."

"In later interviews, Jake did question him about his relationship with Anna," Andrew replied. "His replies suggest that he was very fond of her but that she was unaware of the depth of his feelings."

"So if only Leo had been killed, Russell would have been a suspect," Harry said.

Andrew shrugged. "See what you think when you read the interviews."

"That's everyone, then," Bessie said, looking up from her notes. "I don't feel as if those updates have raised many more questions."

"You'd better have Jake ask Colleen about her relationship with Robert," Charles said. "It's probably not relevant, but at least it will look as if we're doing something."

Andrew made a note. "So far, we want to know if it's possible that the poison could have come from anywhere else. We want to know how the poison was stored and where the syringes could have been obtained. We want to know why Scott didn't simply move rather than continue fighting with Leo and Anna over the extension. We also want Jake to talk to some of the other neighbours to see if it was possible that Scott had other difficulties with Leo and Anna. We also want Jake to go back and talk to four other people who aren't on his short list. What else?"

"It might be useful for Jake to ask Scott about the argument he claims he overheard between Leo and Robert," Harry said. "I'm doubtful it actually happened, which makes me curious just how entrenched Scott is in his lie."

Andrew made a note.

"Did anyone else at the party mention seeing Leo and Robert having an argument, even if they didn't hear what it was about?" Bessie asked. "Didn't Colleen say something about it?"

"She did," Hugh said, flipping through his notes. "She said that she saw Leo and Robert having what looked like an intense conversation, but she wasn't close enough to overhear what was being said. She also said that she couldn't imagine that Leo and Anna would stop supporting Robert, even though it would probably be for the best for Robert."

"So they may well have had some sort of disagreement,

even though none of us believe that Leo told him that they were cutting him off," Bessie said thoughtfully.

"What else could they have fought about?" Hugh asked.

"Robert denied that they'd fought about anything. Maybe Jake should ask him what he and his father discussed at the party, without suggesting that it was an argument," Bessie said.

Andrew nodded. "Anything else?"

"The updates we haven't read yet may answer this, but I'm wondering about Robert's relationship with Roy," John said. "You said that Robert is again barely making ends meet and that Roy refuses to help him. I really want to hear more about that."

"Obviously, there's more in the paperwork I'm going to give you today, but not much," Andrew told him. "I'll ask Jake to clarify their current relationship."

"Now we're back to the matter of Colleen and Robert," Bessie said. "Did their relationship have anything to do with the estrangement between the brothers? Assuming they are actually estranged, that is."

"Is Robert working?" John wondered.

Andrew frowned. "I don't believe so, but I'm not certain. I know that he quit his job as a bouncer as soon as he received his inheritance, but I'm not certain whether he's had to find other employment since or not. I don't remember reading anything in the more recent interviews about that. I'll ask Jake to find out." He made another note.

"I think that's about all for now," Charles said. "I can't help but feel as if we're searching for a needle in a haystack here. If I were Jake, I think I'd just close the case as murder-suicide and try to forget about it."

"I don't agree," Harry said. "Jake is right. Something doesn't feel right. The missing poison bottle is just part of it.

I think he should get another handwriting expert to examine the note again."

"I'll suggest that to Jake," Andrew replied.

John nodded. "Something definitely feels off, but it's difficult, mostly because no one had a motive for wanting them dead, at least not a strong motive. I don't consider Scott's motive strong, especially considering he still hasn't received permission for what he wants to do."

"But he couldn't possibly have known that his other neighbours would protest after Leo and Anna died," Hugh said.

"I don't know about that," Doona said. "I know exactly which of my neighbours would complain if I wanted to add an extension to my property. Only one of them would probably bother to file a formal complaint, as that's all it would take to get any plans turned down, but I know that there would be others waiting in the wings, ready to complain if necessary."

"I can have Jake ask Scott about his relationship with his other neighbours and whether or not he expected them to complain about his plans," Andrew said.

"And he'd be smart to say that he suspected they would, regardless," Charles said. "If he says he knew that they would complain, he'll eliminate his motive for the murders."

"If he knew that they'd complain, why would he even bother applying?" Bessie asked. "I'd like to understand why he kept trying over and over again for five years even though Leo and Anna kept objecting, too."

"He addresses that in one of his later interviews," Andrew told her. "He told Jake that he kept changing his plans, scaling things back, rearranging things, trying to find a plan that wouldn't raise any objections. He claims that the last plan he submitted was one that Leo and Anna had privately agreed to support, but as soon as they died, he withdrew the application. Then he resubmitted his first, considerably larger and more involved application. That's the one to which the neighbours on the other side objected."

"And he's been fighting with them ever since," Harry said. "Surely he could simply talk to them and get their agreement before he submits his next set of plans."

"I don't believe he gets along very well with the neighbours on the other side," Andrew told him.

"Who is living in the Jordans' house now?" John asked. "Did Robert and Roy sell it?"

"They did, almost immediately after they took possession. A property management company purchased it. It's been rented out to three different families over the past five years. The current residents have been there for about six months," Andrew replied.

"I wonder how the property management company feels about Scott's plans," Hugh said.

Andrew shrugged. "I've no idea."

"I really hope that Scott didn't kill Leo and Anna over his extension," Bessie said. "It seems as if it's never actually going to happen."

The group chatted for a while longer about Scott and his continually thwarted plans.

"We aren't getting anywhere," Andrew said eventually. "Does anyone have anything else they want me to raise with Jake?"

"Not yet," John said. "I'm hoping to have more questions once I've actually read the other interviews. Right now it feels as if we're just chasing shadows."

"We've raised a few interesting issues, though," Andrew said. "We'll meet again the day after tomorrow. Hopefully, by then, we'll have had a reply from Jake with some answers to our questions."

Everyone gathered up their things, chatting about

nothing much as they did so. Harry was the first to get to the door. As he reached for it, he turned back to the others.

"We should have dinner together after our next meeting," he suggested. "Either here or in one of the cottages on the beach. What do you all think?"

"I'd like that," Bessie said quickly. It was quite unlike Harry to suggest a social gathering, and she really wanted everyone in the unit to be friends.

The others were all happy to agree and, after some discussion, agreed to meet in Andrew's cottage.

"Helen will be happy to cook dinner for all of us," Andrew said. "Or, if she'd rather not, we can have pizza delivered or some such thing."

"Let me know," John told him. "If she doesn't want to cook, I can bring something from the restaurant across from the station."

"What's there now?" Bessie asked.

"It's a Mexican restaurant," John told her. "But that's just today. It could be something else tomorrow."

They all laughed, but there was some truth to John's words. The restaurant across from the Laxey station changed hands frequently.

"Ready to head back to Laxey?" Andrew asked as everyone else slowly cleared the room, most of them clutching boxes filled with leftover doughnuts.

Bessie finished filling a box of her own and then nodded. "We just need Mindy to be working at the desk on our way out. She's the last person we need to meet."

CHAPTER 9

"Is that Mindy?" Andrew whispered as he and Bessie walked into the large hotel's lobby.

Bessie shrugged. "It might be. I don't think I've ever met Mindy. She's around the right age, though."

Andrew nodded. "Now we just need an excuse to talk to her."

"Good afternoon," Bessie said brightly as they approached the desk.

"Miss Cubbon, hello," the woman replied.

Bessie frowned. "I'm afraid you have me at a disadvantage," she said.

The woman smiled brightly. "Mr. Coventry insists that we all know the names and faces of some of his favourite guests, especially those who visit the hotel regularly. I'm surprised we haven't met before, actually. I've been working here for nearly three years."

"It is surprising that we haven't met, in that case," Bessie replied.

"But I haven't introduced myself," the woman said, flushing. "I'm Mindy Holloway, and if there's ever anything I can do for you, please let me know."

"It's very nice to meet you," Bessie replied. She introduced the woman to Andrew. "If you've been here for three years, you must enjoy your work," Bessie said after the introductions.

"I do, very much, but I also appreciate the flexibility that Mr. Coventry allows me. I love to travel, and he's been very good about allowing me to take extra days off here and there to accommodate my desire to see the world."

"How lovely for you. Have you been many places?" Bessie asked.

"France, Italy, all of Europe, really. I spent a fortnight in Japan last year. That was amazing. I've been to New York City and Las Vegas in the US, too. And Toronto in Canada." She sighed. "There's just so much left to see."

"Are you planning your next holiday, then?" Bessie wondered.

"Not yet. I need to save up some money before I start planning anything. I'm quite desperately broke at the moment, actually. New York City was a lot more expensive than I thought it would be." She flushed. "I should say that I let myself spend far more in New York City than I should have, really. I simply couldn't stop buying tickets for Broadway shows and then buying loads of show merchandise as well."

"But what lovely souvenirs for you," Bessie said.

"They are, at that," Mindy agreed. "But what can I do for you? You didn't come over to the desk to talk to me about my travels."

We did, though, Bessie thought. "We're meant to be meeting with Jasper," she said. "If he has time to speak with us."

"I'll let him know you're here," Mindy said before she

picked up the telephone on the desk. She said a few words into the receiver and then put it down. "Mr. Coventry will be right with you," she said.

The words were barely out of her mouth before the door behind her opened and Jasper rushed out.

"Thank you so much!" he exclaimed loudly. "You've saved me from working on my expenses. It's a horrid, boring, dreadful task, best left for days when I'm already angry at the world."

Bessie chuckled. "I can't imagine you angry at the world."

"You need to be here when I'm fighting with both our chef and Stuart," Jasper told her. "It's even worse when Chef gets Stuart to take his side on something. Stuart and I are partners. He should never take Chef's side in anything. But come back to my office and let's talk."

He ushered them behind the reception desk and through the door that led to a short corridor. Jasper's office was the last one along the corridor. It was a small space with not much more than a desk and a few chairs. Bessie knew that he had another, much larger office elsewhere in the building.

"Have a seat," Jasper told Bessie and Andrew as he shut the door behind them. "I hope you don't mind meeting in here. My other office is being painted."

"This is fine," Bessie assured him.

"We'll just have to speak softly," Jasper said. "I'd hate for anyone to overhear us."

"Have you had any additional complaints about stolen credit cards?" Bessie asked as Jasper settled into his seat behind the desk.

"No, thank goodness," Jasper replied. "In another day or two, I may be able to convince myself that whatever happened is nothing to do with the Seaview. Maybe there was a problem at the airport or the sea terminal or on the ferry."

"Do you know how all of the guests who have had problems arrived on the island?" Andrew asked.

Jasper shook his head. "I didn't think to ask that, actually. Which means it's possible that they all came by ferry or through the same airport."

"Were they all here at the same time?" Bessie asked.

"No," Jasper replied with a sigh. "So they probably didn't all arrive on the same ferry or flight. That doesn't mean that the thief wasn't on the ferry, though. Or at an airport, or whatever."

Bessie nodded. "I know you said one of the guests told you that he'd only used the card here, but the others all said that they'd used their cards all over the island. Were you able to find out where they'd all visited while they were here?"

"I didn't ask that many questions," Jasper told her. "I was too upset to think that clearly. I can ring them all back, but I'd really rather not."

"So that leaves us with seven suspects," Andrew said.

"I only have five," Bessie told them. "I refuse to believe that Sandra or Peter is involved in any way."

"I hope you're right," Jasper said. "I'm very fond of both of them."

"The thing that stood out for me, when Bessie and I spoke to everyone, is that they all need money," Andrew said. "I suppose there isn't anyone in the world who wouldn't be happy with an unexpected windfall, but all seven of our, um, people have at least one reason to be actively looking for ways to bring in additional income."

"Perhaps we need to pay our staff better," Jasper said. "All of them need money? Tell me more."

"I suppose Sandra is the exception," Andrew said, pulling out a notebook and flipping through the pages. "She's the one person who didn't mention needing money when we spoke recently."

"I hope that isn't because she's found a way to supplement her income," Jasper said unhappily.

"She lives with her parents," Bessie said. "I believe they're paying for her classes, and I'm fairly certain that they help her with her other expenses as well."

"And Bessie trusts her, so she goes at the very bottom of the list," Andrew said.

"We should talk about Peter, just to get him out of the way," Bessie said. "I trust him because Sandra trusts him."

"But he did admit that he's bad with money and that he wants to save quite a bit so that he can buy Sandra a ring," Andrew reminded her.

"He did?" Jasper asked. "I didn't realise they were that serious already, but good for them. Perhaps it's time for Peter to get a small bonus, one that would just about pay for that ring."

Bessie smiled at him. "He wants something truly special, but I don't think Sandra will care what he gives her."

"I'll speak to him," Jasper replied. "He's working dinner tonight, and it shouldn't be too busy."

"I'd put him just above Sandra at the bottom of the list," Andrew said. "Bessie trusts him, and I think she's an excellent judge of character."

"Indeed," Jasper said.

"What about Todd?" Bessie asked. "I'd hate to think that he's involved in anything illegal."

"He needs an advocate," Andrew said. "And advocates are expensive."

Jasper frowned. "What's wrong? Or shouldn't I ask?"

"I'd rather not repeat everything that Todd told us," Bessie replied slowly. "It's to do with his mother, though. Todd isn't in any trouble, at least not as far as I know."

Jasper sighed. "He worries a great deal about his mother. I suppose I shall have to start some sort of company-wide programme to help staff pay for advocates should the need arise."

"It's a lovely idea, but you don't need to do that for Todd, not right now, anyway," Bessie told him. "Doncan is going to help him out with his little problem."

"And you're going to pay Doncan," Jasper guessed.

"I will, if it comes to it, but I don't think Doncan will ever get around to billing me for his time," Bessie replied.

"So Todd needed money, but he doesn't any longer," Jasper said.

"But at the time when the credit card information was stolen, he didn't know that Bessie was going to help him," Andrew pointed out. "For what it's worth, I found him very likeable. I'd put him just above Peter on the list."

As he made a note, Bessie sighed. "I hate thinking of any of these people as suspects," she said.

"But that's what they are," Andrew replied.

"Surely you didn't like all of them," Jasper said. "Although, obviously, as I employ them all, I hope you did."

"Let's talk about Al," Bessie suggested. "He admitted to us that he sometimes gambles too much, which was more information than I was expecting in a casual chat."

Andrew nodded. "I did tell him that I was a gambler, though, to start the conversation."

"He wants to go across to watch horse racing," Bessie said. "He was expecting a large win the other night, though, to pay for that."

"He was here for work this morning, and he didn't say anything to me about a large win," Jasper told her. "Maybe he's keeping quiet about his windfall, though."

"I don't think so," Andrew said. "He hinted to me about what he'd wagered. If I'm correct, he didn't win."

"What a shame," Bessie said.

"And I got the impression that he might have spent a bit

more on that particular wager than he could easily afford," Andrew added. "He seemed a bit uncomfortable about the whole topic."

"Does that put him at the top of your list, then?" Bessie asked.

"For now, anyway. We still have several other people to discuss," Andrew replied.

"Colin seems lovely," Bessie said. "And completely overwhelmed by his children. I can't imagine him having time to do anything illegal."

Andrew smiled. "I remember when my children were small. It is very hard work, and babies and small children seem to cost a fortune as well. I can imagine Colin being tempted if someone suggested an easy way for him to make a bit of extra money."

"He wouldn't do anything illegal," Bessie said firmly.

"I'm afraid I don't share your confidence in the man," Andrew told her. "I'm going to put him under Al, but only just."

Bessie shook her head. "I'd trust Colin over Al any day. Let's talk about Sherry. She doesn't seem to know what she wants to do with her life."

"No, and I don't expect her to be here for much longer," Jasper said. "She's eager to move across. I think she expects to have more opportunities there."

"She probably will, but she still has to know what she wants to do with her life," Bessie said. "As far as I'm concerned, you can put her even with Al on your list," she told Andrew.

He grinned at her. "That was where I was going to put her. I thought she was nice, but I don't know that I totally trusted her."

"That leaves Mindy," Bessie said after running through

the suspect list in her head. "We just met her a few minutes ago."

"Where does she go on the list?" Jasper asked.

"She seems very nice," Bessie said. "We talked about her travels. She's been a lot of places already, and she's clearly not finished."

"I don't know how much you pay your staff," Andrew said. "But I'm a bit concerned about the amount of travel that Mindy has done. I know it's possible to travel inexpensively, but she's been to an awful lot of places."

Andrew nodded. "I know she travels on a fairly tight budget, and I know she lives with three other women to save on her day-to-day expenses. She does seem to be able to afford more holidays than most, though."

"I can have another conversation with her," Bessie offered. "Maybe I can find out how she can afford to travel so frequently."

Jasper shook his head. "At this point, I'd rather you didn't," he said. "Unless I get another complaint, I think I'm going to try to forget this ever happened. Stuart and I are talking about finding better ways to deal with credit card transactions, ways that keep the cards away from the staff, but that isn't easy."

"And it might make your staff feel as if you don't trust them," Bessie suggested.

Jasper sighed. "I do trust them, which is why this is so difficult for me. I really hope that the information was stolen from somewhere other than here and that I've worried myself over nothing."

"Let us know if you want us to do anything further," Andrew said. "I'll keep my notes and our list, just in case."

"Thank you for taking the time to speak to everyone involved. I'm really grateful," Jasper said.

"We can do more, if necessary," Bessie told him.

"I'll think about it. Stuart isn't happy with just pretending it never happened, but I still think that's the best way forwards, assuming we don't get any further complaints."

"You might want to have an informal chat with all of your staff about credit card theft," Andrew suggested. "Don't limit it to the people we've discussed. It might be wise to let everyone know that there have been a few complaints and that if the complaints continue, the police will become involved. If someone has been stealing card information, that might deter him or her from continuing."

"But then Jasper will never know who was behind the thefts," Bessie said.

Andrew nodded. "But if no one else reports a stolen card and Jasper decides not to continue the investigation, this might deter anyone who'd tried it a few times and is considering doing it again. That's assuming the thief is actually someone at the Seaview."

"And I appreciate the suggestion," Jasper said. "Stuart and I were talking about doing some extra staff training around the importance of safeguarding credit card information, actually. I don't think everyone on staff truly appreciates how easily card information can be stolen."

"And perhaps one member of staff knows all too well," Bessie said softly.

Jasper walked with them back out into the hotel's lobby. "Thank you again," he said.

"You're very welcome," Andrew replied. "Ring Bessie if you need us to do anything further."

"Thank you. I really hope I don't need to ring Bessie," Jasper replied.

"We'll be back the day after tomorrow, anyway," Bessie said.

"Yes, of course. I think Chef was talking about doing tiny

grilled cheese sandwiches for you. I believe he's tired of the pastry chef getting all the glory."

"Grilled sandwiches?" Bessie asked.

Jasper shook his head. "He saw something on telly about American grilled cheese sandwiches, and he's been talking ever since about making them with different cheeses and other fillings. You'll just have to wait and see."

"Now I'm hungry," Bessie complained with a laugh.

"Now I'm looking forward to our next meeting," Andrew said.

They drove back to Laxey talking about cheese and sandwich fillings.

"I'm off to send a long email to Jake," Andrew told Bessie as they got out of his car. "Shall we have dinner together?"

"I'd like that," Bessie replied.

"Is there anywhere you'd especially enjoy going?"

"How about Onchan? We could have dinner at Dan and Carol's restaurant. Although maybe that isn't the best idea, now that I'm full of doughnuts."

Andrew laughed. "Let's go anyway. We can always bring back leftovers if we can't finish. And maybe this will be the time that you won't enjoy something on the menu."

"I can't see that happening, but now that I've mentioned it, I really want some of Dan's amazing cooking."

"I'll collect you at half five," Andrew told her. "Or maybe slightly later, as that doesn't give me much time to get my email sent."

"I'll be ready at half five anyway. Just come over when you're ready. I assume Helen will be joining us."

"I assume so. I can't imagine her passing up a chance to eat at Dan's restaurant. Remind me to tell her about dinner tomorrow night. She can decide if she wants to cook or not."

Bessie nodded. "And now, I think I need a walk on the

beach. That should burn off a doughnut or two and build up my appetite for dinner."

She let herself into her cottage and took her case file up to her office. After locking everything in a drawer in her desk, she headed back down the stairs for her walk. Aware that she didn't have very much time, she walked briskly past the holiday cottages and the handful of people who were lying on the beach and playing in the sand. Once she was past the last cottage, she had the beach to herself. As she walked past the stairs to Thie yn Traie, she glanced up at the huge mansion perched on the cliff above her. It had been a few weeks since she'd seen her friend Mary Quayle, who lived in the mansion. *I must remember to ring her and invite her around for tea,* Bessie told herself as she walked.

Mary and her husband, George, had purchased Thie yn Traie some years earlier, but Bessie had already known the couple before they'd become neighbours. George was a boisterous man who'd made his fortune across, selling everything from insurance to secondhand cars. Mary was quiet and shy, but Bessie knew that she was smarter and had far more internal fortitude than her husband. The past few years had been difficult ones for the couple, and Bessie could only hope that things were settling back to something approaching normal for them now that they had been back on the island for a while.

After the brutal murder of George's friend and former business partner, the couple had gone on an extended holiday, taking their youngest child, their daughter Elizabeth, with them. They'd been gone a good deal longer than originally planned because Mary had fallen ill while they'd been away. Now back at Thie yn Traie, Mary was slowly recovering under the watchful eye of her husband and their three children, as well as their butler, Jonathan Hooper, whom Bessie had known since his childhood.

Bessie was still thinking about Mary as she turned around and headed back towards home. George had left his business in the capable hands of his two sons while he'd been away. As far as Bessie knew, the three were now working together. Elizabeth had temporarily shut down her party and event planning business when she'd gone with her parents, and Bessie knew the young woman was working hard to get the company back to its former level of success. Aside from her understandable worries about her mother, Elizabeth had other concerns that were keeping her from rebuilding her business. Bessie was lost in thought, trying to work out how to help her friend, when she heard someone calling her name.

CHAPTER 10

"Bessie?"

"Pat." Bessie waved at the man, who was standing behind the last cottage in the row. "How are you today?"

He smiled and then shrugged. "I'm okay, but I need some advice."

"From me?"

"From anyone who might have an opinion," Pat replied with a laugh. He sighed and shook his head. "I'm going crazy, or maybe I've always been crazy but now it's becoming more obvious."

"What's wrong?"

Pat looked up and down the beach and then stepped closer to Bessie. "Didn't you say you have a sister?"

"I do, yes."

"So how do you be a good sibling?" Pat asked. "I mean, what sort of presents do you buy her? How often do you see her? What do you talk about when you're together?"

Bessie shook her head. "I don't think my experiences are

going to help you at all. You told me that you were going to see your sister soon. Is that what this is about?"

Pat nodded. "You know that I spent a lot of time in foster care. So did she, but not the same places that I was. We barely know each other, really, but she wants us to work on all of that."

"What do you want?"

Pat stared at her for a moment and then sighed again. "I'd love to have a chance to get to know her and for us to be a family. I've never really had family, you know? I mean, not family that I knew or talked to or whatever. But I'm terrified that I'm going to mess everything up or that once she meets me she'll decide I'm not worth the bother."

"You haven't had a chance to meet her yet?"

"No. She was going to come across last month, but then something came up at work, and she's really busy with her wedding plans, so I'm not going to get to meet her until I go across for the wedding."

"Which is next month?"

"Yeah, if I go."

"Why wouldn't you go?"

He shrugged. "I hate to leave Maggie and Thomas during their busiest season."

"This is the first year they've had any help at all. I'm certain they can manage for a week or even a fortnight without you."

"Oh, I'm not going for a fortnight. My sister wants me to, but I can't leave Maggie and Thomas for that long. I'm not even certain I want to go for an entire week, but that's what I have booked right now."

"No doubt your sister is looking forward to seeing you."

"I suppose so, but she may change her mind once I get there."

"And you may decide that you don't care for her," Bessie suggested. "It works both ways."

Pat was silent for a moment. "I never thought of that, but I can't imagine not caring for her. She's my sister."

"And you are her brother. Again, it works both ways."

"What if her future husband doesn't like me?"

"Then you'll deal with it in a mature way. There's no rule that says you have to get along just because he's married to your sister."

"She wants me to move closer to them, but I've been working really hard to build my life here."

"Maybe you can talk her into moving here. Or maybe you'll both decide that you're happier only seeing each other very occasionally. Or maybe you'll find that you actually do want to move closer to her and then work to find ways to make that happen."

"I knew you'd be full of sensible advice," Pat said.

"You almost sound disappointed."

Pat chuckled. "I've spent the last two hours worrying myself into a state. What am I going to worry about now?"

"Guests, probably," Bessie said, nodding towards the men, women, and children on the beach.

"Ah, they're no problem. Most of them keep to themselves and just enjoy their holiday. The ones who do complain are easy enough to deal with. I just pretend to be really dumb and then give them Maggie's phone number."

Bessie laughed. "Maggie must hate that."

"She's very good at dealing with complaints, actually. Thomas often feels sorry for unhappy guests and ends up giving them a discount or something, but Maggie usually ends up telling them to stop complaining or leave. Most of them end up staying and keeping quiet for the rest of their stay."

Bessie chose her words carefully. "The thing you don't

want to do is borrow trouble," she told him. "Try not to worry about things that may never happen. I'm certain that seeing your sister again is very stressful, but, if you can, try not to imagine how it might go and simply wait to see what happens when you actually see her."

"I'll try, but it won't be easy. I've imagined our reunion a million different times already."

"And in how many of those imagined reunions did you get along wonderfully and live happily ever after?"

Pat laughed. "Okay, so I need to stop imagining everything going wrong."

"I hope you'll try, anyway. You're simply adding unnecessary stress to your life."

"She sent me a picture," Pat said, reaching into his pocket. He held the small snapshot out to Bessie.

The woman in the picture was smiling as she squinted in bright sunshine. Her hair was long and pulled back into a loose ponytail. She was casually dressed and she looked healthy and happy.

"There's definitely a family resemblance," Bessie said as she studied the picture.

Pat nodded. "She looks so much like my mother that it almost hurts, though."

"I'm sorry."

"Thanks. I think I look more like my dad, which bothers me every time I look in the mirror. I hope it won't bother her."

"I think going to see her is very brave of you," Bessie said. "And I think she's being very brave in wanting to reconnect with you as well. You both had very difficult childhoods. I hope you can find a way to put the past behind you and build a strong relationship as adults."

"Except you'd rather I didn't move back to England," Pat suggested.

Bessie laughed. "I would rather you didn't move back to England, actually. You've done a lot for Maggie and Thomas, and I sleep better knowing that the cottages are occupied all year long by someone I can trust."

"Well, I'm not planning on going anywhere in the short term, aside from my week across for the wedding. I've signed up for a number of classes for the autumn term at the college, and I'm just about ready to take my driving test, too. I've a lot of things I need to come back for and reasons to stay on the island."

"That's good to hear."

They chatted for another few minutes before Bessie noticed the time.

"Oh, goodness, I'm supposed to be ready to go for dinner in five minutes," she said after a glance at her watch.

"With the inspectors from the cold case unit?" Pat asked.

Bessie frowned. "Is everyone on the island talking about the unit already?"

"It was on the front page of the paper today. Dan Ross made it sound as if it's a very big thing for the island."

"He would," Bessie muttered. "But in answer to your question, I'm having dinner with one of the inspectors and his daughter. We won't be talking about any cold cases over dinner tonight."

"I was so busy talking about myself that I forgot that I have lots of questions for you about the cold case unit," Pat said. "I'll ask them the next time I see you."

"I probably can't answer any of them," Bessie warned him. "We told Dan everything that we can share with the public."

Pat made a face. "I've only spoken to him a handful of times, but I'm not terribly fond of Dan Ross. He and Maggie are very close friends, though. But you need to go and meet your friend for dinner. Thanks for taking the time to talk to me about my problems."

"You know where to find me if you need to talk more between now and the wedding, or once you get back."

"Thanks."

Bessie turned and walked away as quickly as she could. After a short while, she looked back over her shoulder and then waved at Pat, who appeared to be watching her. He waved back. Helen was standing outside the door to her cottage when Bessie finally reached it.

"I'm so sorry. I was talking to someone, and I lost track of time," she explained as she pulled her keys out of her pocket.

"It's fine. Dad sent me over to let you know that he's running late. I didn't mind waiting here, as it was better than watching Dad typing and muttering to himself."

Bessie laughed. "Would you care to come in while I freshen up?"

"I'd love that. Anything to avoid going back to the cottage before Dad has finished that email."

Helen sat at the kitchen table while Bessie rushed up to her bedroom to change into something nicer for dinner. After combing her hair and powdering her nose, Bessie headed back down to the kitchen.

"No sign of Dad yet," Helen told her.

"I'd offer you tea, but we're going for dinner soon."

"And we're going to the most wonderful restaurant ever, so I'd refuse even if you did offer me tea. I wonder what Dan is putting on his sample plates today?"

"That's a great question. I've eaten there dozens of times and never had the same sample plate twice."

"I've only eaten there a few times. Tell me what else he's done."

Bessie's stomach was growling loudly by the time Andrew finally knocked on the door.

"We've been talking about Dan's cooking for the last half hour," Helen told him. "And now we're both starving."

"Let's go," Andrew suggested. "I'm starving and also curious as to what is on special tonight."

Bessie didn't watch the speedometer as they made their way to Onchan, preferring to believe that Andrew never exceeded the speed limit.

"Table for three?" the woman at the door asked when they arrived at the restaurant.

"Yes, please," Bessie replied.

"I'm afraid there's going to be a short wait," she said apologetically.

Bessie looked around the crowded restaurant. Every table was occupied, and there were three other parties waiting for tables.

"How long?" Andrew asked.

"Fifteen minutes, maybe."

"We'll wait," Helen said. "I don't get here often enough to pass up this opportunity."

Bessie nodded. "I don't mind waiting."

"Bessie?" a familiar voice called. "You should have rung and let us know that you were coming."

Bessie let Carol Jenkins pull her into a hug. Dan and Carol were married, and also partners in the restaurant. Bessie had met them not long after they'd first arrived on the island, when they'd been running their restaurant out of a much smaller location in Lonan.

"How are you?" Bessie asked the young woman. "And how is the baby?"

"She's not really a baby any longer," Carol said. "She's going to have her first birthday later this month."

"How is that possible?" Bessie asked. "I want to see pictures."

Carol laughed. "As always, I have hundreds, but I'll only show you a few of the best." She reached into her pocket and pulled out a small pile of photographs that she handed to

THE JORDAN FILE

Bessie. "You take a look at Wendy while I go and clear a few tables so you can get some dinner."

Helen and Bessie went through the pictures together while they waited. Carol was back a short while later.

"She's still gorgeous," Bessie told Carol.

"And she looks very clever," Helen added. "She looks as if she's studying the world in every photo."

"She is very clever," Carol agreed. "Or maybe she just seems clever because she's our only child."

"What's Dan doing tonight, then?" Bessie asked as Carol put the pictures away.

Everyone standing around them seemed to stop talking and turn to listen to Carol's reply.

Carol looked around and then laughed. "I've never felt so popular," she said. "Tonight Dan is celebrating squares and cubes."

"Tell us more," someone demanded.

"The main course plate comes with a square of lasagna, a square of shepherd's pie, four small ravioli filled with a blend of four cheeses and topped with a basil and garlic tomato sauce, and a square of fish with chip cubes," Carol replied.

"Yes, please," Bessie said happily.

"What about pudding?" a voice asked.

"Pudding consists of a square of brownie, a cube of vanilla sponge covered in a thick milk chocolate coating, a cube of chocolate sponge covered in vanilla buttercream, and a square of bread pudding with custard."

"What shape is the custard?" Andrew asked with a chuckle.

"Actually, Dan is using a stencil to add it to the plates so that it is a perfect square in to which the bread pudding sits," Carol told him.

"Why am I not surprised?" Bessie asked. "He always does every little thing perfectly."

117

"He tries, anyway," Carol replied. "And now I need to clear a few more tables. I'll be right back."

Five minutes later, everyone around them had been seated. As a party of four got up to leave, Helen beamed at Bessie.

"That might be our table," she said. "I'm so excited to try tonight's specials."

Carol showed them to the table after it had been cleared. "You already know what the sample plate is today. If you don't want that, every item on it is available in a full-size serving. Otherwise, we have our regular menu."

"We all want the sample plate," Bessie told her.

"I should warn you that it is easy enough to cut the fish into squares, but once it has been battered and deep-fried, the shape becomes more irregular. It's driving Dan crazy, but most customers don't seem to mind," Carol said.

"We won't mind," Andrew assured her. "We all know it will taste delicious."

It didn't take long for their food to arrive. Carol shared a few stories about baby Wendy when she wasn't rushing around working. After she brought their pudding plates, she sat down next to Bessie for a moment.

"So what's new and exciting with you?" she asked. "I can't imagine what it would be like to be a part of a cold case unit. I'm not certain I'd want to read police reports about murders."

"They can be very unpleasant," Bessie replied. "But I do feel as if we're doing good work."

"Oh, definitely. Dan Ross said that you've managed to solve a few of the cases you've considered. It must be wonderful knowing that you've put killers behind bars."

Bessie nodded and then frowned as a thought crossed her mind. "This may seem like an odd question, but what do you do when someone wants to pay by credit card?"

Carol looked surprised. "We have a machine that we run the card through, if that's what you mean."

"I suppose that's what I mean," Bessie replied.

Andrew smiled at her. "We were talking about credit card theft earlier," he explained. "A friend of mine had his credit card information stolen recently. He thinks the numbers were copied when he used the card in a restaurant near his house."

Carol nodded. "It can happen. Someone was stealing card information at a restaurant where I used to work years ago. He got caught because he used the stolen cards to order things that he had shipped to his own house."

Andrew laughed. "If only all thieves made stupid mistakes."

"Dan has a friend who owns a restaurant in the UK. He was approached by a man who offered to buy credit card information from him. The guy wasn't offering much per card, but it was a busy restaurant that probably took dozens of cards every day. He could have ended up with a substantial extra income if he'd been willing to break the law. As it is, he rang the police and told them everything," Carol told them.

"Surely his customers would have complained if he had done it," Bessie said.

"They might have, if they'd been certain that the information had been stolen at the restaurant, but it was a busy restaurant on the high street in Birmingham. The people eating there were probably using their cards at several different places during the day. According to Dan's friend, the man who approached him was very convincing when talking about why he'd never get caught."

"I hope the police were able to put that man in prison," Helen said.

"Dan's friend never did find out what happened to him."

She sighed. "And now I really must get back to work. We're hiring, if you know of anyone who is looking for work."

"I can't think of anyone off the top of my head, but I'll keep it in mind," Bessie told her.

Carol nodded. "Dan and I have been talking about trying for another baby, but we can't do that until we have enough help here to keep the restaurant up and running while I'm on leave. Or maybe I'm just using that as an excuse because pregnancy was such hard work."

"It is hard work," Helen agreed. "And your first is still very young."

"I struggled to get pregnant with Wendy, though, so we're afraid to wait too much longer, just in case it takes a long time again," Carol replied.

"Good luck with your difficult decision," Helen said.

Carol nodded and then began clearing the empty plates from a nearby table.

"Did we learn anything from that?" Bessie asked a short while later as she, Andrew, and Helen walked out to the car.

"We learned that Dan's recipe for brownies is insanely good," Helen said. "And that custard can come in a square."

"Everything was very good," Andrew said. "And talking to Carol about credit card theft was interesting. Perhaps Jasper should ask all of the employees if any of them have ever been approached by someone wanting to buy credit card information."

"Surely everyone will just deny it," Bessie said.

"Maybe not, if they said no and didn't give it another thought," Andrew replied.

"Surely, if that had happened, the employee would have rung the police to report it," Bessie said.

"Not everyone is comfortable with ringing the police," Andrew said. "But Jasper did say that he doesn't want to do anything further unless he gets another complaint. I suppose we'll simply have to wait and see what happens there."

"And we're waiting for Jake to get back to you after he talks to the suspects in Wyoming again," Bessie said with a sigh. "What can we do in the meantime?"

"Maybe we could go to the Wildlife Park tomorrow," Helen suggested. "I love zoos, and tomorrow is supposed to be warm and sunny."

Bessie nodded. "It should be the perfect day for the Wildlife Park. If we go in the morning, that will give me all afternoon to read through the updates on the case."

"We can do that," Andrew agreed.

In spite of that plan, when they got back to Laxey, Bessie curled up with the updates and read her way through all of them before she headed up to bed. Her thoughts were swirling as she washed her face and brushed her teeth.

"I still don't know who killed Leo and Anna," she told her reflection. "I don't even know if they were both murdered or not. I don't know who at the Seaview has been stealing credit card information, either. At the moment, I don't feel as if I know much of anything."

She sighed and then crawled into bed. "I know I shouldn't keep talking to myself," she muttered as she snuggled under the duvet. "Perhaps it's an inevitable consequence of having lived alone for so many years."

Not wanting to think about exactly how many years that had been, Bessie shut her eyes tightly and went to sleep.

CHAPTER 11

The day was already starting to feel warm when Bessie woke up at quarter past six the next morning. Her internal alarm didn't usually allow her to sleep that late, but she'd been up past her normal bedtime, going through the case file. Now she rushed through her shower to make up for the extra few minutes in bed. Rose-scented dusting powder always reminded her of the man she'd once loved. She slowed down her pace as she closed her eyes and thought about Matthew Saunders for a moment.

"This isn't at all how my life might have turned out," she said softly as she opened her eyes. If Matthew hadn't passed away while sailing to the island, she probably would have married him and then gone with him back to the US. It was difficult to imagine now how different her life would have looked had Matthew survived.

She was still thinking about the man as she took her morning walk along the beach. They'd known each other for only a few weeks before her parents had decided to return to the island and insisted on taking Bessie with them. In that time, though, she and Matthew had taken several long walks together. Neither of them had much money, and walking together hadn't cost anything. Bessie closed her eyes and then shook her head.

"Time to think about the present," she told herself firmly. She marched past the stairs to Thie yn Traie and then continued for several additional minutes. The warmth of the day made her turn back before she'd reached the row of new houses where Hugh and Grace lived. If it had been a bit cooler, she would have kept walking, as she always enjoyed a chance to visit Grace and little Aalish, who was going to be a big sister in the new year, all being well.

After turning around, Bessie turned her thoughts to the cold case. *Why would Leo have killed Anna and himself?* she wondered. Thus far, they'd failed to identify any reason why the couple might have wanted to end their lives. *Does a lack of motive mean they were both murdered?* Bessie wondered. *And if they were murdered, why?* She sighed and turned her thoughts to the stolen credit cards at the Seaview, but that was equally frustrating. "We're just waiting for someone else to complain there," she muttered under her breath.

That thought led to another. It had been some time since Bessie had seen Maggie, the woman who owned the holiday cottages. "I truly think she's avoiding me," Bessie said as she looked at the row of cottages. A few months earlier, Maggie had been convinced Dan Ross was trying to kill her following a disagreement between the pair. Bessie had urged her to ring the police, but Maggie had refused. The issue had been dropped almost as quickly as it had arisen once Maggie and Dan had reconciled. It seemed likely that Maggie was now embarrassed by her behaviour and was doing her best to stay away from Bessie.

I should ring her and suggest lunch or something, Bessie thought as she approached Treoghe Bwaane. The idea went out of her head as soon as she opened her door because her telephone was ringing. She thought about just letting the answering machine pick up, but her thoughts had made her irritable, and the ringing of the phone was simply making it worse.

"Hello?" she said, resisting the temptation to just put the receiver back down immediately.

"Bessie? It's Jasper, Jasper Coventry."

"Hello. I hope this doesn't mean that you've had another complaint."

Jasper sighed. "Not one, but two more," he said gloomily. "And one of them is quite insistent that he used his card only at the Seaview and nowhere else."

"I am sorry."

"So am I. I'm going to have to ring the police now, I think. Having one or two complaints was worrying, but now it's starting to appear obvious that we have a problem."

"Are the same seven suspects still possibilities?"

"More or less. Todd didn't wait on one of the men, but at this point I'm starting to worry that the information is being stolen in some other way."

"What do you mean?"

"I wish I knew," Jasper sighed. "Let's just say that all seven of the original suspects are still on the list, and I'm considering adding everyone else in the entire hotel to the list, too."

"Bringing in the police is probably for the best."

"Yes, I suppose so, but I'd really rather not. Dan Ross is certain to hear about it. He has sources in every police station on the island. A headline article about credit card theft at the Seaview won't be good for business."

"Is there anything else you can think of that Andrew or I might be able to do to help?"

"You aren't going to be here today, are you?"

"No, not today."

"I'm going to have to think about what I want to do. If I

were to call a meeting for those seven people, would you and Andrew be willing to question each of them?"

"I think that's a job for the police."

"Would you and Andrew be willing to talk to all of them?"

"Talk to them?"

"I'm sorry," Jasper said. "I got one of the complaints late yesterday and the other early this morning, and I'm still reeling. I simply don't know what to do. I'm afraid that this could ruin the business that Stuart and I have worked so hard to build, and I'm starting to doubt my ability to judge people's character as well. I thought I could trust everyone who works at the Seaview, and now it's clear that I can't."

"Ring the police and see what they think you should do next," Bessie suggested.

"And then watch the entire story explode over the front page of the *Isle of Man Times?*"

"Shall I have Andrew ring you? Maybe he'll have some advice as to what to do next."

"That would be wonderful. I'd really appreciate that. I know that I'm grasping at straws, but I'd rather not have to ring the police, not if there's another way to get to the bottom of the matter."

"I'll have him ring you," Bessie promised before she put the phone down. After pacing back and forth across her kitchen for a short while, she put her shoes back on and walked over to the nearest of the holiday cottages.

"Good morning," Helen said when she answered Bessie's knock.

"Good morning. Is your father up yet?"

"He was just in the shower a few minutes ago. I'll go and tell him that you're here."

"Oh, no, please don't rush him on my account. If you could, though, when he comes out, please ask him to ring Jasper at the Seaview."

Helen nodded. "Don't tell me he's had another complaint about credit card thefts?"

Bessie frowned, unaware that Andrew had told Helen about the problems at the Seaview.

"Dad told me everything last night," Helen added. "I asked him why you were both so interested in what Carol had to say about stolen credit cards, so he told me."

"There have been two more complaints," Bessie told her. "And Jasper is quite desperate. He knows he needs to involve the police, but he's afraid that, in doing so, Dan Ross will discover what's happening and write an article that will damage the Seaview's reputation."

Helen sighed. "I'll have my father ring Jasper. Hopefully we'll still be able to leave on time for the Wildlife Park."

"I'll be ready, regardless," Bessie told her.

Back in her own cottage, Bessie curled up with the case file and re-read some of the interviews. She was relieved when someone finally knocked on her door.

"Ready to go and see the animals?" Helen asked when Bessie opened it.

"Yes, please," Bessie replied. "I need a break from, well, everything."

Andrew nodded from the doorway. "I spent several minutes trying to calm Jasper down, but I completely understand why he's so upset."

"Were you able to make any suggestions that might help?" Bessie asked as she slipped on her shoes.

"I told him that I'd ring a few friends of mine, inspectors who work in the various areas where the thefts have been reported. I've been doing this long enough that I have connections just about everywhere in England."

"So Jasper can talk to the police, but not the police on the island," Bessie said.

"I'm actually coordinating things between the various

jurisdictions across and the island's police," Andrew replied. "Dan Ross won't hear anything about it from me."

Bessie locked her door and then followed Helen and Andrew to his car.

"Before we came over, I rang a few people and set up times to talk to them later this afternoon," Andrew continued as he started his engine. "And I made an appointment to talk to John later, too."

"And we're all having dinner together tonight," Bessie said. "We can talk about Jasper's problem over dinner, since Helen already knows all about it."

"Except I'd much rather talk about more pleasant things," Andrew replied with a rueful grin. "We'll see. Maybe I'll learn something from one of my colleagues that will help solve the case."

"That would make Jasper happy," Bessie said.

The drive to the Wildlife Park didn't take long. Andrew parked in the small car park and then they made their way to the entrance. After paying for tickets, they walked through the first set of gates and stopped.

"Which way do you want to go?" Bessie asked Helen.

"Let's save the penguins for last," Helen suggested.

An hour later, after having walked through several enclosures, they stopped in front of the café.

"Is it too early for lunch?" Helen asked.

"I believe they're already serving lunch," Bessie replied.

"In that case, I'm ready to eat it," Helen laughed.

Inside the small building, they ordered sandwiches and cold drinks and then sat at a table along the wall at the back. A minute later, the door to the café swung open and Bessie smiled at the couple who walked into the room.

"Hello," she called, waving.

Sandra Cook and Peter Christian both smiled and waved back at her.

"We'll just order lunch and then join you, if we may," Sandra called.

"Yes, please," Bessie replied.

They'd sat at a table for four, but there was a larger table right next to them, so while Sandra and Peter ordered, Bessie and her friends moved to the larger table. The couple joined them a few minutes later.

"Good morning," Sandra said. "It is still morning, isn't it?"

"It is, yes," Andrew assured her.

"And it's a lovely day," Bessie said. "We don't get that many warm and sunny days on the island."

"We were lucky to get today as our day off this week," Peter said.

"And we usually only manage to get one day off together each month, so we were very fortunate to both get today," Sandra added.

Peter laughed. "Now that Mr. Coventry knows that we're becoming more serious about one another, he's going to try harder to give us the same days off each week. We shouldn't have tried so hard to keep our relationship a secret for so long."

Sandra blushed. "I wasn't trying to keep it a secret so much as trying to be discreet."

"But now that everyone knows, we can hold hands behind the reception desk and everything," Peter said, taking Sandra's hand and squeezing it tightly.

She pulled her hand away and rolled her eyes. "You aren't even meant to be behind the reception desk."

"Here we are," a waiter said, handing sandwiches to Bessie, Helen, and Andrew. "The other two will be ready soon," he promised before he headed back to the kitchen.

"We had dinner last night at Dan's restaurant in Onchan," Bessie said as the man walked away.

"I love it there," Sandra told her. "Does the restaurant

even have a proper name? Everyone I know calls it 'Dan's restaurant' or 'that place with the sample plates.'"

Bessie laughed. "It must have a proper name, but I can't say that I've ever noticed."

"Jasper has been having me work with the chef once in a while so that I can learn the basics, in case we ever need extra help in the kitchen," Peter said. "It's incredibly hard work, working in a restaurant kitchen. I have new respect for what Dan does in his restaurant."

"We were talking with Carol, and she mentioned that one of Dan's friends had been approached by someone who wanted him to steal credit card information," Bessie said, trying to sound casual.

Peter's face lost all of its colour. He inhaled sharply and then looked at Sandra. She was staring at him, an unreadable expression on her face.

"On the island?" Peter asked after an awkward pause.

Before Bessie could reply, the waiter returned with the other two plates. He gave them to Sandra and Peter and then smiled at everyone. "Does anyone need anything else?" he asked.

"No, thanks," Andrew said quickly.

The man shrugged and walked away. As soon as he was out of earshot, Bessie replied.

"No, not on the island. I believe Carol said he was in Birmingham."

Peter let out a breath. "I'm glad it wasn't on the island," he said before picking up his sandwich.

Bessie looked at Andrew, who slowly shook his head. She took a bite of her lunch and chewed slowly, her eyes on Peter. He kept his head down, gobbling his way through his sandwich as if he was in a huge hurry. It wasn't until he was nearly finished that Andrew spoke.

"You'll feel better if you tell us whatever it is you don't want to tell us," he said to the young man.

Peter blushed bright red. "I don't know what you mean," he replied.

"Peter, tell them," Sandra said. "If you don't, I will."

Peter put his last bite into his mouth and began to chew. After washing the food down with his drink, he sighed. "I didn't do anything wrong."

"No one is suggesting that you did," Andrew replied.

"It was just an idle conversation, and I, well, I thought maybe Mr. Coventry was behind it."

"Behind what?" Bessie asked.

Peter sighed again. "About a month ago, maybe a bit more, a man said something to me about credit cards and how easy it was to steal their information. I told him that we were always very careful at the Seaview to protect our customers."

Andrew held up a hand. "Where did you have this conversation?"

"Oh, in the restaurant. He'd just had lunch, and after he'd finished, he'd asked for a manager. When I went over, he told me that he didn't want to give his waiter his credit card because he worried about the information being stolen. That's when I said that we were careful at the Seaview."

Andrew nodded. "And then what happened?"

"Then he said something about the advantages of being a bit more careless. Basically, he told me that he'd pay me if I gave him credit card information from the cards that I processed."

Bessie could hear the tension in Peter's voice. Sandra reached over and took his hand and squeezed it tightly. "You didn't do anything wrong," she said softly.

"I should have rung the police," Peter said. "At first I wasn't even certain what he was saying, though. I thought

I'd misunderstood. He said it in a really roundabout way and I kept trying to work out what he meant. When I realised what he was actually suggesting, I got really angry, though."

"And then he immediately backtracked and told you that you'd misunderstood," Andrew suggested.

Peter nodded. "That was exactly it. He was so insistent that I'd misunderstood that I wasn't even certain what to believe."

"But when Peter told me what had happened, it seemed pretty obvious what the man had been suggesting," Sandra said.

"We were going to ring the police, but the guest had already checked out and presumably left the island," Peter added.

"Besides, it would have been Peter's word against his," Sandra added.

"I thought about talking to Mr. Coventry, but in the end we decided to just keep quiet," Peter said. "It never occurred to me that he might try the same thing at other shops and businesses on the island, but now I'm worried that he may have done just that."

"Or maybe he tried again with someone else at the Seaview," Bessie suggested.

Peter's eyes went wide. "He didn't, did he? Please don't tell me that someone at the Seaview actually agreed and has been stealing credit card information."

Bessie looked at Andrew.

"Jasper has had a few complaints recently," Andrew told them. "It's possible that the card information was stolen from them elsewhere on the island, but it's also possible that it was taken at the Seaview."

"This is all my fault," Peter said angrily. "I should have rung the police before the man even left the restaurant."

"It still would have been your word against his," Sandra said.

"But maybe that would have been enough to stop him from getting someone else to steal for him," Peter replied.

"Or maybe he'd already found someone else," Bessie suggested. "Maybe he'd already talked someone in the Seaview into working for him. Maybe he was just trying to recruit additional, um, staff."

Peter sighed. "He'd been staying at the hotel for two nights by the time he spoke to me. After his lunch the day we talked, he checked out and flew home. I hope you're right. I hope, if he did get someone else at the hotel to work with him, that he'd already recruited them before our conversation."

"The question is, who at the Seaview might have agreed to help him?" Bessie said.

Peter and Sandra exchanged glances.

"I'd hate to think that anyone there would do anything illegal," Sandra said. "Mr. Coventry treats us all as if we were his family. I can't imagine stealing from Mr. Coventry."

"But they aren't actually stealing from Mr. Coventry," Andrew told her. "Some people don't see the harm in stealing from big credit card companies. They reckon that the companies have insurance to protect them and that they expect a certain percentage of their transactions to be fraudulent."

"Stealing is stealing, no matter who you're stealing from," Sandra said firmly.

"Let's talk about a few of your colleagues at the Seaview," Andrew suggested. "Just give me your honest opinion of each of them."

Sandra sighed. "I don't want to get anyone into trouble."

"No one is going to get into any trouble based on this conversation," Andrew assured her. "But I'm working with the local police to try to discover from where the card information was stolen."

"Go ahead," Peter said. "I want to do everything I can to help."

Andrew pulled out his notebook. "Mindy Holloway," he began.

"Mindy is nice, but she's obsessed with travelling," Sandra said. "It's all she ever wants to talk about. I suggested once that she could earn more money for travelling if she went back to school and got a degree, but she told me that she's not interested in having to take classes on top of working."

"I like her," Peter said. "She sometimes has lunch in the restaurant before her shift. Mr. Coventry lets staff eat for a very reduced rate. She's always full of wild stories about the places she's been. I don't believe all of them, but I do think she has a lot of fun when she travels."

"Todd Hoffman?" Andrew asked.

"Is lovely and sweet and would never ever do anything illegal," Sandra said firmly.

"He's a good guy who works really hard," Peter added. "I can't see him doing anything illegal. He said something the other day about not ever even having had a parking ticket."

Andrew made a note. "Colin Payne?"

"Is too tired to remember to write down credit card numbers," Peter said with a laugh. "His kids are everything to him, but they wear him out. He said the other day that he hasn't had an uninterrupted night's sleep since they had their first child six years ago."

"Maybe he's hoping he'll get arrested and be able to get some sleep in prison," Sandra said. Then she blushed. "I'm only teasing. I can't imagine Colin doing anything wrong, either."

"What about Sherry Brady?" Andrew asked.

Sandra opened her mouth and then shut it again before looking at Peter.

He shrugged. "She's not my favourite person, but she does her job."

"Why don't you care for her?" Bessie asked.

Peter shrugged. "She's not certain what she wants to do with her life, but that doesn't stop her from mocking other people who are trying to build their careers at the Seaview."

"And sometimes she's very, very friendly with Peter," Sandra added.

Peter squeezed her hand. "You know you don't have anything to worry about."

"I know, but she knows that we're involved, and she should respect that and stop telling you that you can do better and that she's better," Sandra replied.

Andrew made another note. "What about Al Clarke?"

"Al's okay," Peter replied with a shrug. "All he ever wants to talk about is his successes or failures at the races, but the breakfast crowd seems to like him."

"He's always very nice to me," Sandra said. "He usually stops at the front desk when he comes in, just to say hello, before he goes through to the restaurant. He told me once that he'd never had children, but that he wishes now that he had a daughter like me."

Andrew nodded and then looked up from his notebook. "So, can you imagine any of them selling credit card information to the man Peter met?"

CHAPTER 12

"The Seaview has quite a few other employees," Sandra said.

"Do you think any of them are more likely to be behind the thefts than anyone I've just mentioned?" Andrew asked.

Sandra looked at Peter and then slowly shook her head. "I can't even begin to imagine that anyone at the Seaview has been stealing credit card information," she said. "It's such a horrible thought."

"Peter, is there anyone I haven't mentioned that you think might be behind the thefts?" Andrew asked.

Peter slowly shook his head. "Mr. Coventry takes good care of us, and he makes it feel as if we're all working together to make the Seaview the nicest place on the island to stay or to have a meal. I thought everyone who worked there felt the same way about it, really."

"If you had to pick one of the people whom I just named as being the most likely suspect, which person would it be?" Andrew asked.

Sandra frowned. "Sherry," she said after a moment.

"Al," Peter replied.

The pair exchanged glances.

"I've already told you why I don't care for Sherry," Sandra said. "I didn't mention it earlier, but we took a class together last semester, and I think she may have cheated on the final exam."

"Oh?" Bessie said.

Sandra shrugged. "I can't prove it, but she'd been only just barely passing the class, and then she got a ninety-nine per cent on the final. I'd studied for weeks and only got a ninety. I don't know how she could have cheated, but I suspect that she did."

"Maybe she studied really hard, too," Peter said.

"Maybe, but that was the week that Todd was poorly and she took a lot of extra shifts to cover for him. I can't imagine when she'd have found time to study harder than I did."

"Has she said or done anything lately to make you think that she has more money than she should?" Andrew asked.

Sandra laughed. "All she ever does is complain about how poor she is. She wants to move across, but she keeps telling me that she can't afford to move because her mother won't pay for everything. Apparently, her mother wants Sherry to help pay for a flat and a car and all the things you need when you move to a new area."

"And Sherry doesn't want to help?" Bessie asked.

"Right now, Sherry lives at home, rent-free," Sandra told her. "Her parents paid off their mortgage years ago, so they don't charge her anything for staying there. But if Sherry and her mother move to England, they'll have to rent a flat, and right now both Sherry and her mother don't seem to think they can afford to do that."

"What about Al?" Andrew asked Peter.

He shrugged. "His gambling bothers me. I have a mate who used to bet on everything, from proper bets with a bookie to betting random strangers about the weather or the colour of the shoes of the next person who came into the room. He'd lose a load of money and then he'd win just enough to encourage him to keep going. Eventually, he moved across, and I wasn't all that sorry to see him go."

"And Al is the same?" Bessie wondered.

"He isn't nearly as bad, but he still worries me. I know he works at the Seaview just to fund his gambling habits. I could see him being interested in just about anything else that might add to his gambling budget."

"I can't believe we're having this conversation," Sandra said. "Up until today, I trusted everyone at the Seaview."

"And you may be right to do so," Andrew told her. "As I said earlier, the police are investigating. It's possible that the card information was stolen elsewhere on the island or even further afield."

"Do the police have information about all of the victims?" Sandra asked. "Did they all arrive on the island by ferry or maybe fly through the same airport? Were they all coming from the same place? Did they all shop in the same shop in Douglas or elsewhere while they were here?"

Andrew held up a hand to stop the questions. "I'm certain the police will be asking all of those questions and more, but they aren't sharing that information with me. I'm simply doing my best to coordinate efforts between them and the police here on the island. Jasper is concerned that the newspaper doesn't find out about what's happened."

Sandra made a face. "Dan Ross would love to splash that across the headlines," she said. "I can see it now. 'Seaview Sneak Thief Stealing Credit Card Info,' or something similar. Of course, he'd call into question how Mr. Coventry makes his hiring decisions and make everyone on the island start avoiding the Seaview."

"Yes, well, I'm going to do everything I can to prevent that from happening," Andrew assured her.

"If you all want pudding, you need to order at the counter," the waiter said as he approached. He cleared away the empty plates and glasses on to a tray and then walked away with it.

"We've been here forever," Sandra said.

"It isn't busy," Peter replied, nodding at the otherwise empty room. "Having said that, I do think we should get ice cream before we go."

"Yes, please," Sandra said happily.

"Was there anything else?" Peter asked Andrew.

Andrew shook his head. "You go and get some ice cream and enjoy the rest of your day. If you think of anything that you want the police to know, please feel free to ring Bessie. She can get a message to me, and I can pass it along to the police who are investigating the case."

"We'll think about it," Peter assured him. "We'd both hate to see anything negative about the Seaview in the papers."

"And we both hate the idea of someone stealing from our guests," Sandra added.

Bessie watched as the young couple bought themselves ice cream cones and then left the building.

"That was interesting," Andrew said as the door shut behind them.

"I assume you're going to ring Jasper when we get back to Laxey," Bessie said.

"I am, but first I want ice cream, too," he replied.

They all got double scoops of their favourite flavours and then went back outside and slowly walked around the rest of the park.

"I'm so glad we left these guys for last," Helen said when they finally reached the penguin enclosure. "I just love penguins."

They watched the birds swimming and waddling around together for a short while, before returning to Andrew's car.

"Back to Laxey?" he asked as he started the engine.

"That's probably for the best," Helen replied. "I'm cooking tonight, after all."

"What are you making?" Bessie asked.

"I haven't decided yet. Once we get back to Laxey, I'm going to borrow the car and drive to the shops in Ramsey. I'll decide what to prepare when I see what looks good. Is there something you'd particularly like me to make?"

Bessie shook her head. "I'm happy to eat anything I didn't have to cook myself."

Andrew laughed. "After living on my own for the last several years, I've come to feel the same way."

They talked about food as Andrew drove them to Laxey Beach.

"I'll be back soon," Helen promised as she climbed into the driver's seat.

"What are you going to do with your afternoon?" Andrew asked Bessie.

"I'm going to go back through the entire case file, from beginning to end, and see if I can find anything we've missed." She looked up at the clear sky and then sighed. "But first I'm going to take a walk on the beach."

Andrew grinned. "If I may, I'll join you."

"You know you're always welcome."

There were a few people taking advantage of the beautiful weather to splash in the sea or sit on the sand, but once Bessie and Andrew got past the last of the cottages, they had the beach to themselves.

"How are things between Andy and Elizabeth?" Andrew asked as they walked past the steps to Thie yn Traie.

Bessie shrugged. "I wish I knew. I haven't seen either of them in weeks. The last time I saw Andy was when we went with him to look at that house. Elizabeth has been staying close to home. Rumour has it that Mary had something of a setback with her health."

Elizabeth's party planning business had been a huge success before she'd gone on holiday with her parents. One of the reasons why she'd been so popular was that she often worked with Andy Caine, a brilliant young chef. Bessie had known Andy for his entire life. He'd had a difficult childhood and had spent a lot of time at Bessie's cottage during his teenage years. She'd often acted as something of an honorary auntie to the children growing up in Laxey, and Andy had spent more time with her than most.

Some years ago, Andy had unexpectedly come into a large inheritance, and that had suddenly given him the opportunity to pursue his dream of becoming a chef and owning his own restaurant. He'd spent a couple of years doing a training course in the UK and then returned to the island, eager to find the perfect location for his first restaurant. While he was searching for just the right place, he'd started doing some catering for Elizabeth's business. Their relationship was both personal and professional, and Bessie had thought that the pair were well-suited.

They'd decided to end their relationship when Elizabeth opted to go on holiday with her parents. Once she'd left the island, another woman started a party planning business and a relationship with Andy. She'd told Andy a number of horrible lies about Elizabeth and very nearly convinced him to marry her before her untruths were exposed and she left the island. All of that had happened several months earlier, and Bessie was still hoping that Andy and Elizabeth would find a way to work out their differences eventually.

"That's a shame. Mary is a lovely woman."

Bessie nodded. "I've rung a few times to see how she is, but Jonathan simply promises to let Mary know that I've been asking about her."

Jonathan Hooper was the Quayle family's butler. Bessie had known him all of his life as well, but she understood that his first loyalty was now with his employers.

The pair kept walking for several minutes, chatting as they went along about everything they'd seen at the Wildlife Park.

"I'm starting to get a bit tired," Andrew admitted as the new houses came into view in the distance. "I'm afraid I'm ready to turn around."

Bessie nodded. "We really need to get back if I'm going to have time to read everything again before dinner."

"And even though tonight isn't a proper unit meeting, if I've heard anything from Jake, I'll share it with everyone."

"Except Helen?"

Andrew shrugged. "She won't mind taking a short walk on the beach while we talk about the case, assuming there's anything to discuss."

"It does feel as if we're rather stuck at the moment."

"Bessie? Hello?" a voice called from somewhere above them.

Bessie stopped and looked up, smiling and waving at Elizabeth, who was making her way down the stairs from Thie yn Traie to the beach.

"How are you?" she asked as Elizabeth jumped off the last step into the sand.

"I'm good, thanks. How are you?" Elizabeth replied as she stared out at the sea.

Bessie put a hand on her arm. "How are you?" she asked again as Elizabeth's eyes met hers.

"Fine," Elizabeth said, blinking back tears. "It's just – that is, I'm just – or rather, life is just – it's complicated."

Bessie pulled her into a hug, and she wasn't surprised when Elizabeth burst into tears.

"There's Helen back," Andrew said, sounding a bit desperate. "I'll just go and help her with the shopping."

Bessie watched as he nearly ran back down the beach.

"And now I've scared away your friend," Elizabeth said sadly as she lifted her head. "I'm ever so sorry."

"I'll see him later," Bessie replied with a wave of her hand. "I'm much more worried about you."

Elizabeth drew a shaky breath and then gave Bessie a watery smile. "I'm okay, really. Sometimes I just feel a bit overwhelmed, that's all."

"Let's walk back to my cottage and sit behind it," Bessie suggested.

There was a large rock right behind Bessie's cottage. Its flat top was just the right size for two people to sit together and have a quiet conversation. The pair were silent as they walked. Elizabeth took several deep breaths as she went.

"I'm much better now," she told Bessie once they were settled on the rock.

"Good. Would you care to tell me what's wrong, then?"

"As I said earlier, I'm just a bit overwhelmed right now. Mum caught a bad summer cold, and she very nearly ended up in hospital. Actually, I'm fairly certain her doctor wanted her to go to Noble's, but she insisted on staying home. Daddy hired a half-dozen nurses and assistants and whatnot to look after her, but she prefers my company, and I'd much rather be there myself than leave her with anyone else."

"Is she better now?"

"She's improving slowly, and we're down to three extra staff. She's eager to see you, but that may have to wait for another week or two."

"I can wait, but I'm eager to see her, too."

Elizabeth nodded. "You're at the very top of her list of people who she wants to see, once she's well enough for visitors. If I'm honest, you're also at the bottom of the list, because you're the only person on the list. Mum has always struggled to make friends, and most of the people that she's met on the island since we've been here are simply acquaintances."

"She's a lovely woman, and I consider her one of my dearest friends. I've rung more than once in the past month to check on her."

"Oh, yes, I know, and so does Mum. Jonathan always takes careful notes whenever anyone rings, whether it's someone for Daddy about his businesses or someone for Mum. Usually the people who want to talk to Mum are hoping for a charitable donation for some organisation or other, of course, but she always feels better when she hears that you've rung."

"I will ring more often, then. I was afraid I was annoying everyone when I rang."

"Not at all. It's nice for Mum to know that she hasn't been completely forgotten."

"As if I'd forget her."

Elizabeth nodded and then stared off into the distance. "I wish I could forget some people," she said softly.

"Andy?"

Elizabeth made a face. "He rang me last month and then again yesterday. Apparently, he's found what he thinks might be the perfect place for both his home and his restaurant. The thing is, he wants my opinion on it, because no matter what we've been through personally, he respects me professionally."

Bessie gave careful consideration to her reply. "I hope you respect him professionally as well."

"I know he's a brilliant chef, and he may make a decent businessman, but he's too trusting and he's a complete idiot," Elizabeth said, her voice rising in anger with every word she spoke.

Bessie chuckled. "He was certainly too trusting of Jennifer."

"That isn't even her real name. I can't believe he was dumb enough to believe that she didn't know who he was when they first met. Everyone on the island knows Andy and knows that he inherited a fortune from his grandfather, even though he didn't even know that the man was his grandfather."

"Jennifer was a gifted actress."

"Jennifer was a gifted con artist. She very nearly succeeded in getting Andy to marry her, and then she would have cheated him out of every penny of his inheritance before she would have dumped him and left him."

"But that's all in the past."

"Mum keeps saying that, too. That I need to put the past behind me and try to move forwards. Goodness knows she's had to forget about lots of things my father has done in the past, especially things concerning Grant Robertson."

Bessie nodded. "I've seen the house that Andy wants you to see."

"You have?"

"It belongs to a friend of mine. She's eager to sell it because it's far too large for her. She lives alone."

"I thought Andy said that the house had twelve bedrooms."

"It does."

"And your friend lives there all by herself?"

"She does. Her grandparents built it, expecting to have a large family. Now she's the only one left, aside from one nephew who has no interest in living in the house."

"Would it really work for Andy's business?"

"It's enormous, and there are several entrances. When we toured the house, Andy had all sorts of ideas of ways he could use the various spaces. He said something about turning the ground floor into the restaurant and then using the upper floors for living space."

"You toured the house with Andy?"

Bessie nodded.

Elizabeth sighed. "I don't know what to do."

"Do you want to see the house and help Andy make his decision?"

She laughed. "I'm desperate to see it and to talk to Andy, but I'm still furious with him for believing so many horrible lies about me. I, well, I still care deeply for him, but it hurts so much to know that he actually thought that I was capable of being so dreadful."

"Jennifer had convincing proof."

"You saw the proof she used. I wouldn't have called it convincing."

Bessie nodded. "I'm not going to keep defending Andy's actions. He was wrong to believe Jennifer, and whatever he believed, he should have rung you and spoken to you as soon as the accusations were made. That's all in the past, though, and can't be corrected. What you have to decide is whether or not you can move on from the past."

"I want to help him. I'll be honest, I want to work with him again, too. From what he said, the property in question could be perfect for holding special events once it's been completely remodelled. I can't imagine ever forgiving him enough to resume our personal relationship, but we could do great things together professionally, if I can get past everything that happened."

"When you meet new people, do you automatically assume that they're being nice to you only because you have money?" Bessie asked.

Elizabeth shrugged. "That depends on the people. If they have money of their own, then no, but otherwise, I do wonder."

"And do you think you'd feel the same way if you'd grown up without any money and then suddenly found yourself rich beyond your wildest dreams?"

"I know, I know. Andy isn't as suspicious of other people as I am because having money is new to him. And he's gorgeous, which means women used to chase him even when he was poor."

"What did you say to him when he rang yesterday?"

"Oh, I didn't speak to him. He left a long message with Jonathan, all about the house and how much he thinks I can help and whatnot. I haven't spoken to him since I saw him in your cottage months ago."

"If you decide you want to go and see the house and you don't want to be alone with Andy, I can come with you," Bessie offered.

Elizabeth's eyes lit up. "That's exactly what I need. Someone to go with me and stop me from doing anything stupid. I'll ring Andy back this afternoon and see if we can go and see the house next week."

Bessie stared at her for a moment and then nodded slowly. "Okay, if that's what you want to do."

"Thank you, Aunt Bessie," Elizabeth said as she jumped down off the rock. "I feel so much better."

Bessie watched, amused, as the young woman ran back down the beach towards Thie yn Traie. "I wonder if it will be as obvious to Andy as it is to me just how badly she wants to see him," she muttered as she got off the rock and headed into her cottage.

CHAPTER 13

*B*essie made herself a cup of tea and then settled down in her favourite chair with her case file. She re-read the entire thing, finishing just before it was time to head over to Andrew's cottage for dinner.

"That was a complete waste of time," she told her reflection as she brushed her hair, after she'd returned the case file to its locked drawer. Hoping that Andrew would have answers to at least some of their questions, she put on her shoes and then locked up her cottage behind herself.

As she approached the cottage next door, she spotted Harry and Charles walking down the beach towards her. She waved and then waited until they'd reached her to knock on Andrew's door.

"Good evening," she said to the two policemen.

"Good evening," Charles replied.

"Yes, good evening," Harry said.

"I hope you're hungry," Andrew told them when he opened the door.

"Something smells wonderful," Bessie said after she'd inhaled deeply.

"Lots of somethings," Andrew replied.

"Oh?"

"Good evening," Helen said as she emerged from the cottage's kitchen. "Remind me to never, ever, ever offer to cook dinner again the night after I've been to Dan's restaurant."

Bessie laughed. "That doesn't sound good."

"I hope it will be delicious, but I've made far too much work for myself," Helen explained. "I was walking around ShopFast, trying to decide what to make, but everything sounded good. Then I started to think that if Dan can prepare multiple meals at the same time, why couldn't I?"

"Oh dear!" Bessie exclaimed.

"Exactly," Helen said with a sigh. "Whatever Dan is charging, it isn't enough."

"He does have a much larger kitchen and a staff to help," Bessie said.

"Where were you while I was walking around ShopFast, telling myself that it was all going to be wonderful?" Helen asked. She laughed and then shook her head. "It's all going to be interesting, anyway. I've done my best."

"Should I ask what we're having?" Charles asked.

Helen glared at him for a moment and then laughed again. "We're all friends, so I know that no one will complain if nothing is very good."

"I won't complain," Harry said quickly. "I'm hugely grateful that I didn't have to try to cook anything for myself. The kitchens in these cottages aren't the greatest."

"No, but at least we have a nice new cooker in ours," Helen said. "Of course, I broke the previous one, but that's neither here nor there."

"So what are we having?" Harry asked.

"I made several different things for everyone to pick and

choose from. I tried to come up with a theme, but, really, it's all just stuff you can bung in a pot. I made chicken casserole, beef stew, and tomato sauce with meatballs. I'll make the pasta once everyone is here and I know how many of you want it."

"I want some," Andrew said. "But not too much, as I want some of everything."

"I'll have…" Charles was interrupted by a knock on the door.

Andrew opened it and let Doona, John, and Hugh into the cottage.

"Now that we're all here, I'll take orders," Helen said after everyone had said their hellos.

"Orders?" Doona repeated.

Helen explained about the various options for dinner and then took notes on what everyone wanted from the choices on offer.

"And that was completely unnecessary," she said with a laugh as she tore the sheet of paper out of the notebook. "I should have guessed that everyone would want some of everything."

"Do you need a hand in the kitchen?" Doona asked.

Helen shook her head. "I'll just go and make the pasta and then start filling plates. Once I've filled a few, I'll shout loudly so that people can start collecting them. There isn't room for all of them on the counter in the kitchen."

Andrew poured everyone drinks, and then they all sat together in the small sitting room that overlooked the sea.

"Have you heard anything from Jake?" Harry asked Andrew.

"I have, yes," he replied, glancing towards the door to the kitchen. "If we talk quietly, we can talk about it while Helen is busy elsewhere."

"Before we talk about the case, did you ring Jasper?"

Bessie asked as she suddenly remembered their conversation with Sandra and Peter.

"I did," Andrew replied. "We can talk later about what he had to say."

Bessie nodded and then took a sip of her drink.

"Did Jake laugh when you asked if the poison could have come from anywhere else?" Charles asked.

Andrew shook his head. "On the contrary, he said that it was an interesting question and not one that had ever occurred to him. He's started looking into it, but he prioritised speaking to the various witnesses again."

"And what did the various witnesses have to say?" Hugh asked.

"Let's start with Scott," Andrew suggested. "I'll get copies of all of this for you tomorrow, but for now I'll just summarise everything. According to Jake, he became defensive when asked why he didn't simply move rather than continue fighting to get his extension approved. Apparently he'd spent a long time looking for the perfect house, and, once he'd found it, he didn't want to move. He simply wanted to have a chance to improve the property he'd purchased."

"But why does he need more space?" Doona asked.

"He told Jake that he's hoping to get married and have children one day and that he wants to be certain that his house is ready for whatever happens in his life," Andrew replied.

"What if he falls in love with a woman who hates the house?" Bessie demanded. "Or one who lives in Ohio and wants him to move there? I can't see the point in making that house perfect for a family, not until he finds the woman with whom he wants to start that family."

Andrew nodded. "Jake reported that he said something similar, but Scott just sighed and made some comment about the police grasping at straws all these years after Leo killed his wife and himself. He told Jake that he can't imagine why his plans are at all interesting to the police."

"I hope Jake talked to the other neighbours and they had horrible things to say about him," Doona said.

Andrew chuckled. "He did talk to some of the other neighbours, but none of them said anything outright horrible. Jake spoke to three other people who live on the street, people who've been there since before Leo and Anna died. He said they were all polite about Scott, but he got the impression that none of them cared for the man. Having said that, they all also said that they didn't really care if he added an extension or not."

"So he didn't talk to the people right next door," Bessie said.

"Not yet. They are on the list for tomorrow."

"What did he have to say about the argument he claims he heard between Robert and Leo?" Harry asked.

Andrew looked down at his notebook. "Apparently, it all happened too long ago now for Scott to remember any of the details. He told Jake that he remembers that there was an argument, but that was all he was willing to say now that so much time has passed."

"Interesting," John said. "I'd be more suspicious of him if he'd claimed to remember the conversation, really."

Harry nodded. "That was a smart way to get out of what was probably a lie."

"I'm ready to start serving," Helen announced from the kitchen's doorway. "If one or two of you could help, it will go a lot faster."

Doona and John made their way into the kitchen while the others moved over to the small dining table in the corner of the room. Doona emerged from the kitchen a few minutes later, carrying two plates piled high with food. John was right behind her with two more. It took them only a few minutes to serve everyone. Then they went back into the kitchen to get bowls of salads and plates of crusty bread and buttery garlic bread. Helen was the last one out of the kitchen, carrying her own plate as she appeared.

"This is delicious," Bessie said after her first bite.

"Which thing?" Helen asked.

Bessie grinned at her. "That was chicken casserole, but I'm certain it's all going to be good."

Over dinner, they talked about restaurants and why more of them didn't serve sample plates the way that Dan did. Eventually everyone finished eating.

"I've three options for pudding, too," Helen said. "But I didn't make any of them myself."

"I'm too full to think about pudding right now," Andrew said.

"Maybe we should all take a walk on the beach before we have pudding," Bessie suggested.

Doona and Helen cleared the table, and then the entire group went out for a walk. They'd gone only a short distance when Bessie felt a few drops of rain.

"So much for our nice day," she said, looking up at the fast-moving clouds above them. "I think we need to get back inside quickly."

The skies opened just moments after they'd all rushed back into Andrew's cottage.

"So much for walking off a few calories before we eat anything else," Doona said.

"Maybe we should continue the conversation we were having before dinner," Harry suggested.

"That must mean it's time for me to go to my room," Helen said with a laugh. "I'll be back out in an hour to make tea and coffee to go with pudding."

"Perfect," Andrew replied.

The others all settled into seats in the sitting room as Helen left the room.

"Where were we?" Hugh asked.

"I think we'd covered most of what Scott said," Andrew replied. "And what the other neighbours said about Scott."

"What about Robert?" Bessie asked. "Is he working, and what's going on between him and Roy?"

Andrew opened his notebook and turned a few pages. "Robert is not working. He hasn't worked since his parents died, but he did tell Jake that he's starting to think about looking for a part-time job. He told Jake that he didn't need to work, but that he was getting a bit bored being at home all the time. Jake reckoned that he's running out of money but doesn't want to admit it."

"What about his relationship with his brother?" Hugh asked.

"Jake said that when he asked about Roy, Robert just shrugged and said that they'd had some difficulties over the years and that once their parents were gone, neither of them saw any point in pretending otherwise."

"So they aren't in contact at all?" Bessie asked.

"According to Robert, he sends his brother a card for Christmas and his birthday and that's about all the contact that he needs. He did admit that he doesn't get cards back, though."

"So Roy isn't making an effort to stay in touch," Bessie said.

"Apparently not," Andrew replied.

"I wonder how many times Robert asked Roy for money before Roy stopped speaking to him," Harry said.

"Jake is going to talk to Roy tomorrow," Andrew said. "He's interested in hearing his side of the story."

"So are we," Bessie said.

Andrew nodded. "Of course."

"Did Jake ask Robert what he and his father discussed at the party?" Doona asked.

Andrew nodded. "And he said something similar to what Scott had said. Basically, he claimed that the conversation was too long ago for him to remember the details. He told Jake that it broke his heart that he couldn't remember, because that was the last conversation he'd ever had with his father, but at the time it hadn't seemed significant. He said they probably talked about his job and maybe some of the little things that needed to be done at the house. Robert told Jake that he often went over and changed light bulbs and washers in leaky taps and that sort of thing for his parents."

"And did he have anything to say about his relationship with Colleen?" Bessie wondered.

"Jake asked Robert if Roy had minded that his brother was involved with his former girlfriend. Robert just laughed and said that Roy and Colleen had been apart for a really long time by the time he took her out for the first time. He said Roy couldn't have cared less about Colleen by that time."

"How does he know that if he isn't speaking to Roy?" Hugh asked.

Andrew shrugged. "That's a good question, actually, but not one that I think we'll be able to get answered – not in the short term, anyway. Jake doesn't want to have to go back and speak to anyone again in a hurry."

"I don't blame him," John said. "But we are going to have more questions."

Andrew nodded. "Let's wait until we have the rest of the answers from the first list of questions before we worry about coming up with any others. Jake has a full day of interviews scheduled for tomorrow. Maybe something interesting will come out of those interviews."

"Tomorrow," Bessie said. "And they're how many hours behind us?"

Andrew glanced at his watch and then sighed. "I said tomorrow, but, actually, it's today that he'll be talking to everyone. Time zones are confusing. He's actually probably interviewing someone as we speak, but he won't send the results until after we're all in bed tonight. I should have more information for you all at the meeting tomorrow."

"Is that all from what he did today, then?" Hugh asked. "Or was it yesterday?"

"It was yesterday, because I sent the email full of questions before I went to bed, and he started working through it immediately," Andrew replied. "He sent his reply before he went to bed last night, but I didn't get it until I logged into my email this afternoon."

"And that's everything?" Harry asked.

"He did manage to speak to three of the four people who we suggested might need a closer look," Andrew told them. "As I said, you'll all get copies of the interviews, but, from what Jake has told me, he's not convinced that any of them are serious suspects."

"What about the fourth person?" John asked.

"Ah, he's moved away and is now living in California," Andrew replied. "Jake has sent an email to a colleague there, and that colleague is due to speak to the man tomorrow, or rather, later today."

He looked up as Helen stuck her head into the room.

"I hate to interrupt," she said. "But I can hear the Victoria sponge calling to me from the kitchen. It's only just possible that it's the jam roly-poly, of course. They sound similar when I'm imagining things."

Everyone laughed.

"We're just about done, anyway," Andrew told her. "If you go and start a pot of coffee, we'll be finished by the time it's ready."

Helen nodded and then went into the kitchen.

"Does anyone have anything to add?" Andrew asked.

"We still have a number of unanswered questions," Bessie said.

Andrew nodded. "Let's hope those answers are more helpful than the ones we've had so far."

"This may be the first case we can't actually solve," Harry said. "I have to say, as disappointing as that will be, we've done amazingly well so far. We shouldn't be surprised if we can't solve them all."

"I think the biggest problem with this case is that we still aren't certain whether it was murder-suicide or just murder," John said. "And I'm not certain we'll ever get any closer to answering that question."

"The coffee is ready," Helen announced.

Bessie got to her feet and followed the others into the kitchen. While she knew that Harry was right, that they weren't going to be able to solve every case they considered, it still bothered her that this one might go unresolved. She wasn't certain why, but she believed that Leo and Anna had been murdered, and she wanted justice for them.

"Victoria sponge, jam roly-poly, or chocolate Swiss roll?" Helen asked everyone as Andrew began pouring cups of coffee.

"Yes, please," Bessie and Doona said at the same time.

"I can do that," Helen assured them.

A short while later, they were all back around the dining table, this time with plates full of cakes in front of them. Harry had opted for a very small slice of jam roly-poly, but everyone else had agreed to have a bit of everything.

Bessie took a bite of Victoria sponge and sighed. "It's delicious, but I really want to solve this case."

"Maybe this one will simply take a bit longer," Andrew said. "Maybe, after we're done, Jake will keep poking at it for years to come until he finally finds the solution. We have only a fortnight to consider the case, but it won't be closed after those two weeks. Jake will keep working on it for the rest of his career, and it will remain open forever, unless it's solved."

Bessie nodded and then took a big bite of her chocolate Swiss roll. "It would still be nice to solve it tomorrow," she said after she'd swallowed.

Everyone around the table nodded.

"Let's talk about something more pleasant," Harry suggested. "Have I ever told you about the time I caught a serial killer entirely by accident?"

Bessie laughed. "Only this group would consider a serial killer in any way a pleasant topic of conversation."

"But he caught him," Hugh said. "That's the important thing."

The next hour flew past as they all enjoyed cake and coffee and the various police inspectors took it in turns to talk about some of their former cases. After Bessie and Doona helped Helen fill the dishwasher, everyone got ready to leave.

"How is Grace?" Bessie asked Hugh before he reached the door.

He sighed. "She's suffering with morning sickness again, and it's much worse this time because last time she could simply stay in bed all day if she needed to. Now, Aalish demands attention whenever Grace tries to rest."

"It's going to get worse when the baby arrives," Andrew told him. "Aalish is going to want attention constantly until she gets used to having to share her parents with the baby."

"Grace's mum has already offered to come and stay with us for a few weeks once the baby arrives. She's told Grace that she'll either devote herself to Aalish and ignore the baby or devote herself to the baby so that Grace can still give Aalish lots of attention. We're still talking about it."

Bessie grinned. Grace's mother had almost taken over when Aalish had first arrived, and eventually the new parents had had to send her home so that they could raise Aalish their way. Perhaps they would be less quick to get rid of the woman the second time around, though.

"I'm just going to walk Bessie home," Andrew told Helen.

"I can walk Bessie home," Harry offered. "I'm going out into the rain anyway."

Bessie frowned at the light rain that was falling. "You don't want to walk any farther than you have to. I'm quite capable of walking home by myself."

"But you'll let me escort you to your door, because I like to pretend to be a gentleman once in a while," Harry said with a wink.

Bessie laughed and then nodded reluctantly. A few minutes later, she and Harry reached her door.

"And now I need to double-check that everything is in order," Harry said after Bessie opened the door. "Andrew insisted on it."

Bessie might have argued, but some years earlier, while she was in the middle of a murder investigation, someone had broken into her cottage and created an enormous mess. Nothing had been taken and no real damage had been done, but the entire incident had made Bessie more cautious about leaving her cottage empty at night. She now also felt slightly less annoyed whenever her friends insisted on checking that the cottage was empty when they brought her home.

So she stood in the kitchen and listened to the footsteps as Harry stomped around on the floor above her. He smiled at her when he walked back into the kitchen.

"I'll see you at the meeting tomorrow," he told her. "Good night."

"Good night," she replied. "And thank you."

CHAPTER 14

*B*essie was on her way back to her cottage the next morning when Andrew waved to her. He was standing just inside the sliding doors to his cottage, sipping a cup of something.

"Good morning," Bessie said brightly.

"Good morning," he replied. "I had a long conversation with Jasper this morning. He's asked that we come over to the Seaview around eleven for a meeting with all of the possible suspects."

"Was he very upset when he heard what had happened with Peter? I hope he isn't angry that Peter didn't tell him about it at the time."

"He was unhappy, but not terribly surprised. He's been in the business for a long time and seen this sort of thing before. He also understood why Peter didn't say anything, although obviously he wishes that he had."

Bessie nodded. "I suspect if Peter had said something, that Jasper would have talked to every single member of staff about the man. He might well have been able to prevent his current problems."

"Yes, well, he'd already spoken to Peter before I rang and, as I said, he understood why Peter didn't tell him. Peter will be at the meeting, as will Sandra, but Jasper has already assured them that they aren't suspects."

"That's good to hear. It's still going to be awful, though."

Andrew nodded. "But hopefully we'll be able to help put a stop to what's happening before the Seaview's reputation is damaged."

"What are you planning to do with your morning, then?" Bessie asked.

Andrew shrugged. "I hadn't really given it any thought. What about a trip into Ramsey? We can wander around the shops for a short while, buy a few books, and then drive over to the Seaview."

"That's an excellent idea. We were just there, but I'm certain I'll still find books I'll want today, too."

Not only did the bookshop carry a huge selection of books, cards, and gifts, but they also kept a list of Bessie's favourite authors and regularly sent her boxes full of new releases from those writers. In spite of that, though, she still enjoyed nothing better than spending a half hour browsing the shelves herself.

"I'll finish my coffee and then get ready to go. I'll meet you at the car in twenty minutes," Andrew told her.

Bessie nodded and then walked briskly back to her cottage. She combed her hair and changed into what she'd planned to wear for the meeting later. It seemed unlikely that they'd return to Laxey before the meeting, not if they were having lunch at the Seaview. She was standing next to Andrew's hire car, watching two small children chase each other across the sand, when Andrew joined her.

"They're enjoying the nice weather," Andrew remarked, nodding at the children.

THE JORDAN FILE

"It's another lovely day, at least so far. It does look as if it might rain later, though."

Andrew looked at the clouds in the distance and shrugged. "We'll be indoors for much of the day, so I suppose it doesn't matter to us."

"They'll be disappointed, though," Bessie said, laughing as the older child splashed into the sea and then immediately ran back out again, shouting loudly about how cold the water had been.

"Were you expecting bath water?" his mother asked, smiling and shaking her head.

Bessie and Andrew got into the car, and he slowly drove away.

"Who is at the top of your list of suspects, then?" Bessie asked as they left Laxey.

"Either of the two that Sandra and Peter identified. Al or Sherry seems the most likely to me."

Bessie nodded. "I hate suspecting any of them."

"Imagine how tempting it would be, though. All you have to do to make a bit of extra money is write down a few numbers and pass them along. Who doesn't want a bit of extra money?"

"Wanting extra money is one thing. Stealing to get some is another."

Andrew parked in the car park for the bookshop. The pair spent half an hour looking at books and they both purchased several. After leaving their books in Andrew's boot, they walked up and down the high street, mostly window shopping. They did go inside a few charity shops, where Bessie found two more books she wanted, and Andrew found a CD he'd been trying to find for years.

"It will be just my luck that it won't play for some reason," he said as they left the shop. "It isn't scratched at all, but you never know with CDs."

"I definitely don't, as I don't have any way to play them."

Andrew laughed. "I was about to ask if your car had a player, but clearly not."

Bessie had never learned to drive. She'd spent some years relying on the island's buses to get her where she needed to go, but then a friend of hers had opened a small taxi service in Laxey and offered her discount prices for using his service. He'd sold the company years later, but the Douglas-based service that bought it still gave Bessie bargain pricing. The service was very useful to her, although she often received rides from friends as well.

"Does your hire car? You could check it on the drive to the Seaview."

"The CD cost a pound. I'm not going to return it, even if it doesn't work. I'll leave checking it until I get home."

They got back to Andrew's car with just enough time to get to the Seaview for their meeting with Jasper.

"I'm not looking forward to this," Bessie said as Andrew pulled out of the car park.

"Neither am I. I believe Jasper is expecting someone to confess, but that may be unrealistic of him."

Andrew parked near the door, and then the pair slowly made their way across the car park.

"I'm dragging my feet," Bessie admitted.

"Let's just go and get it over with," Andrew said in a determined voice.

Jasper and Sandra were behind the reception desk as they entered the lobby.

"Hello," Jasper said glumly.

"Hello," Bessie replied.

"Everyone is here," Sandra said. "We're just waiting for Carla to come and take over the reception desk."

"Carla?" Bessie asked.

"She's the housekeeping manager and she's never worked

behind the reception desk before, but we aren't expecting anyone to check in before midday, and most of the people checking out have already left," Jasper said. "She was the only person I could find to cover for Sandra while we have our, um, little chat."

"I'm here, and I'm terrified," the young woman said as she walked towards them. "Are you quite certain you want me to do this?"

Jasper nodded. "You'll be fine. We're only going to be in the meeting room, just a few steps away. Text me if you need me."

Carla took a deep breath and then nodded. "I'll be fine," she said unconvincingly.

Jasper gave her a quick hug before he looked at Bessie and Andrew. "Let's go," he said flatly.

They followed him and Sandra to the door with a sign that read "Staff Only." Jasper opened it and then gestured for the others to go ahead. Sandra led them down the short corridor to another door. She tapped on it before she opened it.

Bessie followed her into the room. It was a small conference room with a rectangular table at its centre. The other six suspects were sitting around the table. Peter looked miserable, but the others mostly just looked confused. From what Bessie could see, neither Al nor Sherry looked worried.

"Everyone have a seat," Jasper said.

Bessie sat down next to Sandra, who'd taken a seat next to Peter. He immediately took Sandra's hand. Jasper sat next to Bessie and Andrew took the seat on his other side. For an awkward moment, no one spoke. Then Jasper cleared his throat.

"It's come to my attention that we had a guest around six weeks ago who attempted to get one of my staff to steal credit card information," he said.

A few people around the table gasped.

"Obviously, that person refused, and eventually that person came to me and told me the story," Jasper continued. "What I want to know now is whether any of you were approached."

People exchanged glances and looked around the room. For several seconds, no one spoke.

"I had a guest say something sort of odd at reception one day," Mindy said, breaking the tense silence.

"What did he or she say?" Jasper asked.

"He – it was a man," Mindy told him. "He was checking in, and as I put his credit card through, he asked me if we kept any records of the card numbers or anything. I told him that we just swipe the cards and then immediately give them back to our guests and that he didn't have to worry about his card information being stolen here."

Jasper nodded. "That was a good answer."

She flushed. "I started thinking about it later, and I realised that we do write down numbers when people make bookings over the telephone, but he hadn't asked about that. Anyway, after I gave him his card back, he said something about how people were making a lot of money stealing credit card information. I said that I didn't know how they slept at night. He, well, he sort of smirked at me and then turned around and walked away."

"It may well have been the same man, trying to gauge how willing you might be to join his little enterprise," Andrew said.

"Thinking back now, it feels more suspicious than it did at the time," Mindy said. "At the time, it was just another slightly odd conversation. We have a lot of those at reception."

Sandra laughed. "You can say that again."

"Is that what he was going on about?" Al asked. "If we're

talking about the same man, or even if we aren't, I suppose, I did have a rather odd conversation with someone about credit cards. He said something about how valuable they were and I agreed that they made life a lot easier. Then he said that people could make a lot of money with them, if they knew what they were doing. I just laughed and said that the credit card companies were the only ones making money from credit cards. He started to say something else, but then he just shrugged and that was the end of that."

"When was this?" Andrew asked.

"Maybe six weeks ago, probably a bit longer," Al replied.

"Anyone else?" Jasper asked.

A few people shook their heads. Jasper sighed and looked at Andrew.

"What should I do?" he asked.

"I think you should ring the police and let them question everyone," Andrew replied.

"The police?" Todd said. "Has someone done something wrong?"

"I'm not talking to the police," Sherry said. "I thought we were all one big happy family here. Not much of a family if you ring the police."

Jasper nodded. "I'd rather not involve the police, but I've reason to believe that one of you is withholding information from me. I've done everything I can to investigate, but I'm not getting anywhere. I may have to bring in the police."

"Has someone broken the law?" Colin asked.

"I believe so," Jasper told him. He sighed and then looked at Andrew again. "I'm probably doing this all wrong."

"Indeed," Andrew said.

Jasper sighed. "I do think of all of you as family," he told the others. "And that's why this is so very difficult for me. I've had seven complaints in the past few days from guests who had their credit card information stolen from them while they were staying at the Seaview."

Bessie studied the surprised faces, trying to work out who was only pretending to be surprised. Al slowly shook his head, while Sherry looked more angry than shocked. Todd and Colin both appeared stunned, and Bessie was worried that Mindy might burst into tears.

"In that case, surely the police are already involved," Colin said.

"They are, but across several different jurisdictions because the crimes were all reported by our guests once they'd returned home," Jasper explained. "But the police on the island are also involved. I was hoping to find the culprit myself. I really wanted to give him or her a chance to explain, but it looks as if I'm going to have to just sit back and let the police investigate."

"Where would they even start?" Sandra asked.

"They'll start by looking to see who came into contact with each of the guests who has complained," Jasper told her. "That's why I've invited all of you to this meeting. Each of you interacted with all seven of the guests who've complained."

"But we all interact with dozens and dozens of guests every day," Sherry said. "And there are several other members of staff as well."

"Yes, and I'm certain the police will want to speak to everyone who works here," Jasper said. "But as I said, one member of staff had already reported being approached by the man who may well be behind the whole thing, and now we know that Mindy and Al were approached by him as well. The staff member who was approached first was able to go through our security camera footage and find the man in question. I'd like Mindy and Al to look at the footage and see if it's the same person who had those unusual conversations with each of you."

Mindy nodded. "I'd be happy to do that."

"Sure," Al said.

"If we can positively identify the man, then we can go back through our records and see who waited on him in the restaurant and who checked him in and out of his room," Jasper said. "And the security footage from all of our cameras will show us exactly which members of staff interacted with him during his stay."

"That won't prove anything," Sherry said.

Bessie thought the young woman was starting to look a bit nervous.

"It should help narrow down the list of possible suspects," Andrew replied. "If one person waited on the man in the restaurant and then later waited on every guest who has complained, well, that would be very suggestive, at least."

"I wait on a lot of guests every shift," Sherry argued.

"Once the police have compared who interacted with the suspicious guest and who interacted with the guests who have had their data stolen, they'll be able to put together a short list of suspects," Andrew said. "Those suspects will be questioned and then investigated."

"The people who work at reception will have interacted with everyone," Sherry said.

"Thanks," Sandra said.

"As I said, the police will look at everyone who works here," Andrew replied. "But Mindy has already admitted to having had a conversation with the man. She's now a witness, rather than a suspect."

"I spoke to him, too," Sherry said quickly.

"Oh?" Andrew replied.

She nodded. "I waited on him, and after he'd eaten, he gave me his card and said, 'Take good care of this.' I just laughed and then took the card to Peter, because that's what we do in the restaurant. After Peter processed it, I took it back with the slip for the man to sign and he said something about how people could make lots of money if they took an extra minute to take notes on the credit cards that they saw."

"And what did you say?" Andrew asked.

"I asked how that worked because I could use a bit of extra money. I thought maybe he was talking about some sort of market research or something. When he made it clear that he was talking about stealing card information, I told him I wasn't interested," she replied.

"Why didn't you say that ten minutes ago when Mindy and Al were talking about the man?" Jasper asked.

Sherry shrugged. "I didn't think it mattered."

"Since it was clear to you what the man wanted, you should have told me about it when it happened, actually," Jasper said. "Clearly, I want to know when someone comes to my hotel and asks my staff to break the law for him."

"It isn't as if the credit card companies can't afford to lose a bit of money," Sherry replied.

"We all pay more for everything we buy in order to help make up those losses," Colin said.

"It isn't just about money, either," Andrew said. "A lot of innocent men and women have to deal with a great deal of inconvenience, reporting their cards stolen and then having the cards cancelled."

"Yeah, well, I said no," Sherry muttered.

"Did you?" Jasper asked, staring hard at her. "Did you really?"

Sherry flushed. "I need to go," she said. "I have a doctor's appointment."

"You're on the schedule for lunch today," Jasper said.

"Oh, yeah, I'm not going to be able to work today," she

replied as she reached the door. "I may not be in tomorrow, either."

She pulled the door open and rushed out of the room.

"Shouldn't you stop her?" Colin asked. "I thought she was acting very guilty just then."

Jasper nodded and then sighed. "Someone will stop her before she gets far. As I said earlier, the police are investigating."

The meeting broke up a few minutes later. Everyone seemed shocked and subdued by what had happened. Bessie and Andrew walked with Jasper and Sandra back to the reception desk.

"It's been very quiet," Carla said happily when they arrived. "I hope nothing is wrong. Sherry looked very upset when she walked through here a few minutes ago."

"Everything is fine," Jasper assured her. "Thank you for your help."

"I was happy to do it," Carla replied.

"What's going to happen now?" Jasper asked Andrew as Carla walked away.

"I'll ring John Rockwell and tell him about the meeting. I suspect someone from his office will want to interview Sherry before the end of the day," Andrew replied.

Jasper sighed. "Now I'm stuck hoping it was her because I simply want the investigation to be over."

CHAPTER 15

Andrew and Bessie sat in a corner of the lobby while Andrew rang John. After they'd spoken, John had Bessie repeat what she could remember of the conversation, too.

"I'll see you both at two," he told Bessie when she was finished.

"We've had some interesting answers from Wyoming," Andrew said as Bessie handed back his phone. "Jake is just about finished with our first list of questions."

"That's good. I just hope we can come up with some additional questions once we've had these answers. Otherwise, I think we're stuck."

"Ready for lunch?" Jasper asked. "I'm going to join you, because otherwise I'll keep annoying poor Sandra, who is simply trying to do her job."

Bessie smiled sympathetically at him. "I know you're worried about Sherry and the stolen credit cards, but you need to try to put it out of your mind while John is investigating."

"Maybe something has gone disastrously wrong in the

kitchen, and I can fill my time shouting at the chef," Jasper replied.

"Or you could just have a nice lunch with us," Bessie said. "And stay far away from the kitchen."

Jasper and the Seaview's chef had a famously difficult relationship. Bessie had heard more stories than she could remember about the arguments that they'd had over the years. For a long time she wondered why they continued to work together if they disliked one another so much, but lately she'd begun to suspect that they both enjoyed arguing, too.

In the restaurant, Peter showed them to a table near the windows. Bessie looked out at the sea and sighed happily.

"I never get tired of watching the water," she said.

"It's lovely," Jasper agreed. "And it's never the same from moment to moment. I should spend more time watching the water and less time worrying."

After a delicious lunch, where Bessie did everything she could to keep the conversation light, Jasper walked her and Andrew to the penthouse conference room.

"Just biscuits today – oh, and a few leftover mini muffins from a breakfast meeting," he told them as they walked into the room.

"They're wonderful," Hugh said around a mouthful of muffin.

Bessie frowned at him and then walked to the back of the room and filled a plate with a few muffins and a biscuit. Then she poured herself a cup of tea and found a seat at the table.

"Did you get any of the lemon ones?" Hugh asked. "Those are my favourite. They're lemon and poppy seed and they're delicious."

By the time everyone else arrived, Bessie had tried all of the different flavours available. She and Hugh gave the others their opinions as they all filled plates. Harry simply poured himself coffee before taking his seat, but everyone else tried at least a few of the small treats.

"Where should we start?" Andrew asked as he opened his notebook. "We were waiting for Jake to talk to one other person who wasn't on his short list. That man is now living in California. Jake had a colleague there speak to him. You'll all get copies of the interview, of course, but Jake and I both agreed, after reading this most recent interview, that the man seems even less likely as a suspect."

They talked about the man for a few minutes before Andrew moved on.

"Jake went and spoke to the neighbours on the other side of Scott," he said. "They are the ones who are now objecting every time he submits plans for an extension. According to Jake, they didn't bother to object while Leo and Anna were alive, because they knew that Leo and Anna would do so. Once Leo and Anna were gone, though, they knew they'd have to do something. Apparently, they don't want Scott to alter the house in any way, not even with the smallest of additions, and they plan to object every time he files anything until he finally gives up and stops asking."

"Or sells his house," Doona suggested.

"Or sells his house," Andrew agreed.

"Is that how it works in the US, then? You request permission to do something and if one of your neighbours objects, you can't do it?" Bessie asked.

Andrew shrugged. "I've no idea. From what I know of the US, though, it's probably different in every town, city, county, or whatever. It certainly seems, in this instance, that the objections are getting his plans rejected every time."

"Did they have anything else to say about Scott?" Bessie asked.

"They don't care for him, and they're hoping he'll move

away," Andrew replied. "Jake got the impression that they don't really care about the extension. They simply want to get rid of Scott."

"Why?" Bessie asked.

"Jake tried to pin that down, but they were vague," Andrew replied. "If we think it matters, I can have him go and talk to them again."

"I'm not certain it matters," Harry said. "The couple in question didn't really know Anna and Leo, did they?"

"They claim they didn't know them at all, that they knew their names only because they saw them on the various objection letters that were sent to protest Scott's extensions."

"How did they see the letters?" Doona asked.

"The plans and objections are all a matter of public record," Andrew explained. "Jake said they all get printed in the back of the local paper."

"Can anyone think of any possible motive for them for the killings?" Harry asked.

"Maybe they're lying about knowing the Jordans," Hugh said. "If that's the case, they could have had any motive imaginable."

"But if they didn't know the Jordans, it's difficult to see why they would have killed them," Charles said. "Is that everything from Jake?"

"There was one more thing. Jake went back and talked to Roy. He asked him a few questions about his younger brother and their relationship. At some point in the conversation, Roy let slip that Robert is getting financial help from Russell."

There was a moment of surprised silence.

"Why would Russell be helping out Robert?" Doona asked eventually. "I know he was fond of Anna, but from everything I've heard, Robert inherited quite a lot of money. Why should Russell care if Robert spent it all very quickly and is now struggling?"

"That's a very good question," Andrew said. "One that Jake is going to put to Russell later today."

"Is it possible that Russell is Robert's father?" Hugh asked.

Everyone looked at him.

"Roy was the one who said that his mother and Russell were close friends," Hugh said. "And you all have to admit that the brothers don't actually look very much alike, at least not in the pictures that I've seen."

Andrew frowned. "It's an interesting theory. If we run with it, can anyone see why that would give Russell a motive for killing Leo and Anna?"

"Maybe she'd never told him that Robert was his son. Maybe he found out another way and was furious with Anna for keeping the secret from him," Doona said.

A buzzing noise interrupted. John frowned and then pulled out his phone.

"Hello?...I see...Okay, thank you," he said before putting his phone back in his pocket.

"Sorry about that," he told everyone. "I'll just quickly tell you that Sherry has confessed to stealing credit card information from a number of guests here. She's backtracked on her earlier statement and is now insisting that she just thought he was doing market research or some such thing with the numbers she was providing, but no one believes her."

"Poor Jasper will be very upset," Bessie said.

"But also relieved," Andrew told her. "And if she's confessed, maybe she'll also agree to try to help the police find the man who recruited her in the first place."

"That would be helpful," Bessie said.

"Now, where were we?" Andrew asked. "We were talking about..."

Another phone buzzed. Everyone laughed as Andrew pulled his out of his pocket. "It's Jake," he said, sounding surprised. "I'll just take it in the corridor, so you don't have to listen to half of a conversation."

"What if we want to listen?" Doona murmured as Andrew left the room.

While he was gone, everyone helped themselves to more muffins and drinks. Bessie even managed to persuade Harry to try a blueberry muffin. When Andrew walked back into the room, he was smiling broadly.

"There's been a breakthrough," John guessed.

Andrew nodded. "And Bessie did it again."

"There was another possible source for the poison?" Hugh asked.

Andrew sat down and then flipped back through his notebook. "Sorry, Jake had a lot to say, and I want to be certain I get it all right."

Bessie took a sip of her tea and then ate a vanilla muffin while she waited for Andrew to find his place in his notebook.

"Right, here we are," he said eventually. "First of all, Jake feels as if he's an idiot for not thinking about the issue himself. He knew that Leo had retired from a lab, so when the autopsies showed poison, he immediately checked to see if it could have come from that lab. When he discovered that Leo not only had access to the poison, but that it was kept in a location that was accessible to many people, he simply assumed that the poison must have come from that lab."

"But now he's learned otherwise," John said.

"He's learned that there might be another explanation," Andrew replied. "When we asked him to find out if it was possible that the poison had come from somewhere else, he gave that job to a new recruit. The new guy is rather desperate to prove his worth, so he went digging on an epic scale. Those are Jake's words, by the way."

"And what did he find?" Bessie asked as Andrew took a sip of tea.

"Apparently, the lab where Leo had formerly worked is the only place in the state that anyone can get that particular combination of chemicals," Andrew replied.

"That's rather disappointing," Hugh said.

"But the new recruit had a vague recollection of a shop that used to sell science equipment – chemistry sets and microscopes and that sort of thing," Andrew continued. "He'd been really interested in chemistry when he was younger, and he remembered the shop having hundreds of bottles of different chemicals."

"And he thought maybe someone bought the necessary chemicals and mixed up his or her own supply of poison?" Doona asked. "Where would someone get the recipe for something like that?"

"Jake is still working on that, but he has managed to discover that the shop in question did stock everything that would be needed to mix up the poison that was used," Andrew replied.

"Did stock?" Harry repeated. "They aren't still in business?"

"They are not. They closed about ten years ago after they were raided by the police for stocking a large number of illegal items," Andrew told him.

"Such as?" Harry asked.

"A lot of drug paraphernalia and quite a lot of drugs, apparently," Andrew said. "The manager was dealing on a large scale and using the shop as a front. Allegedly, the owners didn't know anything about what was happening in their shop. They were never charged with anything, but the former manager is still in prison."

"And among the drugs and whatnot, they also found poisonous chemicals?" Bessie asked.

"They found a huge variety of chemicals, many of which were dangerous, some of which were not meant to be available to the general public. The owners were buying everything from a large chemical company in Mexico and importing it without completing all of the required paperwork. It shouldn't have been allowed into the country, but it managed to get through somehow."

"But they still weren't charged with anything?" Charles asked.

"They claimed that the sales representative from the chemical company had assured them that it was all safe and legal. In their defense, they'd made no effort to hide what they were doing. The bottles and jars were all on display in the shop, clearly marked with the exact names of the chemicals inside. From what Jake could determine, the manager didn't have any idea what he was selling and, from the shop's records, it doesn't appear as if they were selling all that much of anything, either."

"So anyone could have wandered in and bought the supplies necessary for making the poison, but also an explosive device or maybe some sort of deadly gas," Harry said.

"It sounds that way, anyway," Andrew replied. "Fortunately for everyone in Wyoming, no one seems to have done any of those things. The shop was closed down and the inventory was confiscated. Most things were destroyed, but a large box with samples of some of the merchandise was kept as evidence."

"And from your smile, I'm going to guess that something in that box has something to do with our case," John said.

"Bessie also asked about the syringes," Andrew said. "They were fairly common syringes, the sort that you can find in medical supply shops, but Jake had always been unable to work out exactly where they'd come from. None of the local medical supply shops sold syringes with the exact same brand stamp on them. He sort of assumed that they'd been purchased out of state somewhere."

"But there were some in the evidence box from the closed science shop," Doona guessed.

"There was a small box of them in the evidence box from the closed science shop," Andrew told her.

"So now we know that there might have been another source for the poison, and we know where the syringes came from," John said. "Does all of that get us any closer to finding out what happened to Leo and Anna?"

"The manager went to prison, but no one else at the shop was ever charged with anything," Andrew said. "And that includes the assistant manager."

"Scott," Bessie guessed.

Andrew nodded. "Scott was the assistant manager of the science shop."

"He did have the strongest motive for killing Leo and Anna, even if I can't imagine killing someone over an extension," Doona said.

"And he did try to shift suspicion to Robert by claiming to have heard him arguing with his father," Bessie added.

"But where did he get the recipe for the poison?" Harry asked.

"Jake is still working on that question," Andrew said. "He's having Scott brought in for questioning, based on the discovery that the syringes that were used match the ones that were taken from the science shop. He's hoping that Scott might break down and confess when he finds out that the police have made that connection."

"Scott has had five years to come up with a cover story," Bessie said. "He'll tell Jake that Leo used to buy things from the shop all the time, or that Robert was once their best customer."

"You could be right, and I suppose it's possible that Leo and/or Robert did patronise the shop, but for right now I'd put my money on Scott being behind the deaths."

"Over an extension?" Doona said, shaking her head.

The group talked for a while longer, but it quickly became clear that they were just talking in circles.

"All we can do now is wait until Jake gets back to me," Andrew said as everyone began packing up their things. "I'll keep you all informed, but I don't think we need to schedule another meeting for now."

"I'll be heading back to London tomorrow, then," Harry said. "I've been asked to consult on a rather important case that I'm not allowed to discuss."

"I think I'll go back tomorrow, too," Charles said. "For once, I'm not working on anything else. It might be nice to just sit in my flat and do nothing for a day or two."

"You could do nothing here," Bessie suggested.

Charles smiled at her. "It's a tempting thought, but Laxey Beach is a bit busy at the moment. Every time I look out my window, I see a small child falling into the sea or a teenaged boy skipping stones. Believe it or not, London will feel quieter because the crowds there are far more impersonal."

Bessie gave both men hugs before they left the room. Then she hugged all of her friends as well.

"What now?" she asked Andrew as they got back into his car.

"Maybe we should both curl up with our new books and relax for tonight."

"That's a lovely idea."

A WEEK LATER, Andrew knocked on Bessie's door as she was getting ready to go out for her morning walk.

"You're up nice and early," she said.

"Jake rang me late last night. I sent an email to everyone else, but you don't have email."

"Perhaps I should get a computer."

"But then I'd miss getting to tell you what's happened," he replied.

Bessie slid on her shoes and then she and Andrew began a slow stroll along the beach.

"I talked to Jasper last night," Bessie said before Andrew could begin. "Apparently, in exchange for leniency, Sherry has agreed to tell the police everything she knows about the man who was buying the card information from her."

"She isn't still working for the Seaview, is she?"

"Jasper is prepared to give her another chance, but apparently she's given him notice. She and her mother are going across, and she's going to look after her sister's baby for a year or so. She told Jasper she's really happy to be getting away from dealing with people all day."

"I suppose that's all good news, then," Andrew said.

"Does that mean that you don't have good news from Wyoming?"

"I have sad news from Wyoming. Apparently, Scott still had some of the poison and some syringes left. He ended his life early yesterday morning."

"Oh dear. That is very sad."

"He left a note behind, one that Jake is certain is genuine. What's interesting is how similar his handwriting is to Leo's."

"Really?"

"Jake had an expert take a look, and she's fairly confident that the note that was supposed to have been written by Leo and the note that was definitely written by Scott were both written by the same person."

"So Scott killed Leo and Anna?"

"He admitted as much in his note."

"Over his extension?"

"According to the note, it wasn't just that. He and Leo had more history than anyone realised n. Apparently, when he was just nineteen, Scott did an unpaid internship at the lab where Leo worked. According to Scott's note, Leo taught him all about poisons and dangerous chemicals over the six months while he was there."

"Why didn't Jake know about that?"

"Because Scott never told him, and no one else seems to have known. It's possible, maybe even likely, that Anna knew, but she isn't here to tell us. Russell was on sabbatical during the six months in question."

"What about Roy?"

"He was working in a different building at that time. He told Jake that he and his father didn't really talk about work and that he couldn't remember his father ever mentioning any interns, even though we know that Leo worked with several over the years."

"Did something awful happen during those six months, then, that made Scott hate Leo?"

"Scott was vague in his note, but it appears that something happened, something that made Leo reluctant to write a letter of reference for Scott. His note rambles on a bit, but it seems that Scott blamed Leo for a lot of the negative things that happened to him after that."

"What happened?"

"Scott dropped out of college and went to work in a shoe shop. Over time, he went back and earned a business degree, but in the letter he claims that chemistry was always his first love and that Leo had stolen that from him."

"Because he wouldn't write him a letter of reference?"

"Because without the letter, Scott didn't get selected for

some special programme that he'd hoped to do. As I said, the letter rambles, but it seems as if Scott never got over that missing letter, and he blamed Leo for the fact that he was managing a clothing shop instead of working as a chemist."

"So he killed him many years later."

"He said he never planned to kill him, but that eventually he couldn't stand it any longer. He was furious that Leo had ruined his life, and now he couldn't even build an extension for his chemistry lab because of Leo."

"He wanted to build a chemistry lab?"

"He did, and he had quite a lot of equipment in boxes, ready to be used once the lab was up and running."

"Things he'd taken from his previous job," Bessie guessed.

"Exactly that." Andrew sighed. "I can give you a copy of Scott's letter, if you want to read it. He also recorded a video of himself reading the letter and then, well, it shows him injecting himself with the poison."

Bessie shuddered. "How awful."

"He said in the video that he didn't want there to be any doubt as to what had happened to him."

"So we've closed another case," Bessie said after they'd walked in silence for several minutes.

"We have. I wonder if we could consider something a bit less distressing next month. Maybe I can find a simple forgery case or a stolen hatbox."

"A stolen hatbox?" Bessie echoed.

Andrew shrugged. "You never know."

THE KELLER FILE

AN AUNT BESSIE COLD CASE MYSTERY

Release date: October 6, 2023

Andrew is back on the island for the next cold case unit meeting, and this time he's brought his son Matthew along. When Andrew shows Bessie the stack of listings he's been sent by his island-based estate agent, Bessie is shocked to see that one of her friends has put her house on the market.

A quick call reveals that the friend's telephone is out of service, which is worrying. While Bessie does what she can to find her friend, the cold case unit has a missing person case of its own to consider. A young woman and her two-year-old daughter vanished ten years earlier. The question is, did they leave voluntarily or did something awful happen to them?

With two missing person cases to solve, Bessie is busier than ever in this eleventh book in the series.

A SNEAK PEEK AT THE KELLER FILE

AN AUNT BESSIE COLD CASE MYSTERY

Release date: October 6, 2023

Please excuse any typos or minor errors. I have not yet completed final edits on this title.

Chapter One

"I'm sure Dad's complained about me a lot," Matthew Cheatham said.

Elizabeth Cubbon, known as Bessie to everyone, shook her head. "Not at all. He doesn't talk about his family very often." She wasn't lying. Andrew didn't tell her much about his family, although she had heard a few things about Matthew.

"He'd be justified in complaining about me, really," Matthew told her with a sigh. "I should be old enough to take care of myself, but here I am, staying with my father so he can look after me."

"I was under the impression that you were here to look after your father."

Matthew laughed. "Yes, okay, we're looking after each other." He sighed again and then waved a hand at the sea in front of them. "He thinks that being by the water will be therapeutic."

"I agree. I credit the sea air and my daily beach walks with keeping me fit and healthy."

"And if you don't mind me saying so, you've lived a long time."

Bessie bristled. "I'm in the later stage of middle age, but I certainly wouldn't say that I've lived a long time."

"Later stage of…." Matthew trailed off and then smiled. "I hope I can continue to be as healthy and vibrant as you are as I get older."

The pair fell silent for a moment as they sat side by side on the rock behind Bessie's cottage on Laxey Beach.

"I should be grateful that my father brought me along on his holiday, really, shouldn't I?" Matthew asked eventually.

"I believe he isn't meant to be travelling on his own at the moment."

"But he usually brings Helen. I love my sister dearly, but I wouldn't want to stay in a cottage on the beach with her for a fortnight."

"I think Helen is lovely."

Matthew nodded. "She is lovely, but she never cared for my second wife, and I can almost hear her thinking 'I told you so' whenever I say anything about my divorce."

"That must be difficult."

"It is. Dad didn't care for my second wife, either, by the time we separated, but he was very supportive when we first began seeing one another. But I promised myself I wasn't going to talk about her or about my divorce. Tell me your life story instead."

What is keeping Andrew? Bessie wondered, glancing up the beach towards the holiday cottage where he and

Matthew were staying. "I'm afraid I've led a rather dull life," she said.

"My father said that you've lived in your cottage for a really long time."

"I bought it when I was eighteen, and it's been my home ever since. I can't imagine living anywhere else."

"Eighteen? I didn't have ten pounds to my name when I was eighteen, let alone enough money to buy a house."

Bessie nodded. "I inherited a small sum, enough to allow me to purchase the cottage. Houses on the island were considerably less expensive in those days, of course. And my cottage was quite a bit smaller as well. I've added two extensions in the years since I bought it."

"So you grew up on the island?"

"Actually, no, I grew up in Cleveland, Ohio, in the United States."

Matthew stared at her. "Really? Then how did you end up owning a cottage on the beach on the Isle of Man?"

Bessie glanced behind them again, but there was no sign of Andrew anywhere. "I'll give you the short version," she said with a chuckle. "I was born on the island, but, when I was two, my parents decided to emigrate to the US. We moved to Ohio, where some of our family was already settled. We were there for fifteen years before my parents decided to return to the island."

"When you were seventeen?"

"Yes, when I was seventeen. My older sister, who was nineteen, stayed behind. She and the young man she'd been seeing for over a year got married very quickly. My parents refused to allow me to remain with her or to marry the young man I'd been seeing."

"I would have been furious."

Bessie laughed. "I was very angry. They practically had to drag me on to the ship for the journey back to the island. I spent the entire sailing sobbing in our cabin. I thought my heart was broken and that I'd never get over losing Matthew."

"His name was Matthew?"

"It was, Matthew Saunders."

"Did you call him Matt?"

Bessie shook her head. "We hadn't been seeing one another for very long, really. I was still referring to him as Mr. Saunders most of the time. I'd only dared to use his Christian name once or twice. We were much more formal in those days, of course."

"Everyone calls me Matt. Matthew feels formal to me. But I interrupted. You cried all the way back to the island. How did you go from that to owning your cottage?"

"We'd only been back on the island for a short while when I received a letter from Matthew. He'd decided he couldn't live without me, so he was coming to get me. I was almost deliriously happy for the next few weeks as I waited for his arrival."

"I'm sorry. I can tell this isn't going to end well. You don't have to tell me anything else."

Bessie shook her head. "Everyone on the island knows the story. I don't mind telling it, really, although it's still painful, even though many years have passed."

Matt patted her arm. "I should have had my father tell me about his friends on the island, shouldn't I? Then I wouldn't have had to ask awkward questions. I've been rather self-absorbed lately, and it never occurred to me to ask him about the people I'm going to meet while I'm here."

"I'm certain he'll be happy to tell you about everyone he knows here. But let me finish my story. Matthew didn't survive the voyage. He passed away just a few days before his ship was due to dock in Liverpool. Before he'd left the US, he'd written his will and, in it, he left all of his possessions to me. His parents were kind enough to sell his things and send me the money. It wasn't a great deal of money, but it was enough to allow me to purchase my cottage, which was essential because I blamed my parents for his death and couldn't bear living with them any longer."

"I'm so sorry," Matt said. "Your parents must have felt terrible, too."

Bessie frowned. "They may have. They probably did, actually, but I was too angry to care how they felt. I regret it now, but after Matthew's death, I never spoke to them again."

Matt was silent for a moment. "And you've lived on your own ever since?" he asked eventually.

"I have. There was another man who once proposed to me years ago, but he lived in Australia, and I found that I loved the island too much to agree to leave. I can't imagine how different my life would have been if I'd married him and moved halfway around the world."

"I've been to Australia. It's beautiful and the weather is amazing, but I wouldn't want to live there."

"No one could complain about the weather here today."

Matt looked up at the cloudless sky and nodded. "Summers in England are usually very nice. It gets a lot hotter in Australia."

"All the more reason to be glad I stayed here."

"Don't you get lonely, though?" Matt sighed. "Sorry, that's probably a rude question. I'm just struggling a bit. I'm living on my own for the first time in a long time, and I find myself just wandering around my flat, feeling lonely."

"I quite enjoy being on my own. I suppose, over the years, I've become quite accustomed to my own company. I can't imagine sharing my cottage with anyone, really, and I also can't imagine living anywhere else."

"Maybe, if I give it some time, I'll come to enjoy living alone. There are some advantages. I get to eat what I want and watch whatever I want on the telly, but I'm not very good at looking after myself. I tend to eat too much rubbish and watch too much football."

"I don't even have a television."

Matt stared at her. "What do you do all day?"

Bessie laughed. "I read a great deal. I'm also something of an amateur historian. I work with the librarian at the Manx Museum on various different projects. At the moment, she's having me catalogue several boxes of old papers, most of which haven't seen the light of day in a very long time."

"That sounds interesting, but surely after a long day of cataloguing, you'd enjoy watching a sitcom, or maybe a drama."

"Maybe, but you don't miss what you've never had. Buying my cottage took nearly every penny that Matthew had left me. My advocate invested what was left on my behalf. I've been fortunate enough to have been able to live ever since on the income that those investments generated, but for many years I had to be very frugal. By the time I felt that I could afford to buy a television, I'd found other ways to fill my time."

"What sort of books do you read?"

"Mostly murder mysteries, although I'll read just about anything if I'm desperate. In the days when I first moved into my cottage and money was very tight, I used to borrow most of my books from friends, and I'd read whatever they were willing to lend me. I visited the library in Douglas as often as I could, but it was a bus journey away and I didn't always have bus fare."

"I suppose you didn't have a car."

"I've never owned a car. I never learned to drive. For many years, I relied on the island's buses and trains, but when a friend of mine opened a small taxi company in

Laxey, his service was a good deal more convenient. Because we were friends, he gave me special rates, and by that time my investments had grown to the point where I could afford to indulge in taxis rather than buses for most journeys."

"And you aren't tempted to learn to drive now?"

Bessie laughed. "I do think about it from time to time. My friend sold his company to a large Douglas-based one. They still give me a substantial discount, but I've not always been fond of all of their drivers. Having never even attempted it, the idea of driving a car is quite terrifying, though."

"I can teach you to drive while I'm here. I taught my kids. You can't be any worse than they were."

"It's a tempting offer, but I think I'll stick to taxis and friends."

"You know where to find me if you change your mind."

Bessie nodded. "You brought your car with you, didn't you?"

"Dad flew over, but I came on the ferry with my car. I'm not fond of flying and I'm even less fond of hire cars." He glanced over his shoulder at the car that was parked in the small parking area outside of Bessie's cottage. "And I'm very, very, very fond of my car."

Bessie looked over at it and shrugged. "I'm afraid cars all look rather alike to me."

"I won't bore you with any of the details, but believe me when I say that she's something special."

"At least you won't be stuck in the cottage when your father is busy elsewhere."

"Exactly. Dad has his hire car and I have my own car. We can both come and go as we please."

Bessie looked back up the beach. *What is keeping Andrew?* she wondered. She didn't mind chatting with Matt, but she'd much rather have Andrew there to help keep the conversation flowing.

"So, tell me about the other people who will be at dinner tonight," Matt said after a minute. "Dad told me that he's invited all of his friends from the island so that they can all meet me."

"I believe everyone from the unit has been invited, along with a few other special guests. Your father has reserved a private dining room at the Seaview for us."

"I've heard the Seaview is gorgeous. Helen said she wants to stay there some day."

"It's the nicest hotel on the island, and the restaurant does wonderful food."

"I hope you don't think I'm being nosy, but I'd love to hear a bit about the people I'll be meeting later. It's difficult being the only new person in a group of people who've known one another for years."

Bessie nodded. "I understand."

"Dad told me that I'd be meeting John, Donna, and someone else, a young police constable, but I've forgotten his name already. I'd be grateful if you could tell me about each of them, especially the constable's name," Matt said with a sheepish grin.

"The constable is Hugh Watterson," Bessie said with a laugh. "He'll be the young man who looks no more than fifteen, even though he'll be at the dinner with his wife and daughter."

"Hugh Watterson, got it. I'm afraid if you tell me what his wife and daughter are called, I'll forget."

"His wife is Grace and his daughter is Aalish, which is the Manx form of Alice."

"What a lovely name. I don't think I'll forget that. Am I remembering correctly that Hugh is in school at the moment?"

A SNEAK PEEK AT THE KELLER FILE

"He's gone back to school to earn a degree. He's doing everything he can to advance his career now that he's married with a family."

"How old is Aalish?"

"She'll be two in December. Grace is expecting again. She's due in February."

"What an exciting time for all of them. I hope they have lots of extra help around. In my experience, grandparents are excellent at helping out."

Bessie nodded. "Both sets of grandparents are very involved."

"What about Donna, then?"

"It's not Donna, it's Doona, which is another Manx name."

"Thank goodness I asked! I'd hate to get it wrong. Doona, right, I'm going to remember that. Tell me about Doona."

Bessie grinned. "Doona Moore is somewhere in her forties. We met in a Manx language class, years ago now. She was working towards ending her second marriage and she'd moved to Laxey for a complete change of scenery. I believe she was hoping to meet other people around her age in the class, but she was the only person under the age of sixty taking the class."

Matt laughed. "I have a friend who did that same thing once. He signed up to take a class, hoping to meet women, but the entire class was just other men who'd all signed up for the same reason. He dropped out after the first session."

"Luckily for me, Doona stayed and, over time, we've become very close friends. She used to work for the Laxey Constabulary at the reception desk, but she quit working after an unexpected inheritance."

"How very fortunate for her."

"I'm not certain she'd put it that way. It was her second

husband who passed away. They were separated, but not divorced, when he died."

Matt frowned. "That sounds vaguely familiar. Is his murder the one that my father got involved in at the holiday park in the Lake District a few years ago?"

Bessie nodded. "That was where your father and I met. He was staying in the cabin next door to the one that Doona and I were sharing. Doona was a suspect in her husband's murder, and your father was kind enough to help us get through the investigation."

"And then Doona inherited something from the dead man?"

"He'd never rewritten his will after he and Doona separated. I believe he continued to hope that they might be reunited one day. Doona inherited his entire estate, which was substantial."

"Did my father tell me something about him owning part of the holiday park?"

"He did own part of the holiday park, and now Doona owns his share and spends a great deal of her time managing it from a distance."

"That sounds difficult."

"It is difficult. Obviously, summer is their busiest season. She actually went across in July to help out, and only returned to the island yesterday. I'm looking forward to seeing her later."

Bessie turned her head and looked up the beach again. While she was enjoying her conversation with Matt, she'd prefer it if Andrew joined them sooner rather than later.

"That just leaves John. I believe he's an inspector with the local constabulary."

"He is. Inspector John Rockwell is also in his forties. He and Doona have been involved with one another for some time now."

"Good for them. I assume from the name that Doona is from the island. Is John?"

"No, he moved to the island from Manchester. He and his wife were hoping for better opportunities for their children."

Matt frowned. "I think I missed something. He has a wife? I assume she's an ex-wife, if he's involved with Doona now."

"Sorry, I didn't mean to confuse you. When John first moved to the island, he brought his wife, Sue, and their two children, Thomas and Amy, with him. Sue hated the island, though, so after a year she returned to Manchester with Thomas and Amy."

"That must be tough for John. How old are the kids?"

"It was difficult for John. Thomas and Amy are teenagers, and he missed them terribly when they were in Manchester. Fortunately, they weren't there for long."

"Oh? Did they decide they wanted to live with John instead?"

"No." Bessie sighed. "I don't know why I'm hesitating. Everyone on the island knows the story."

"You don't have to tell me anything. I can always ask Dad to fill me in."

Bessie laughed. "And, of course, your father knows the story, too. Basically, Sue very quickly remarried. She'd never stopped loving one of her former boyfriends, and they'd crossed paths again when he began treating her mother for cancer during the year that Sue was living on the island."

"He was treating her on the island?"

Bessie shook her head. "I'm telling this badly. He was in Manchester, and so was Sue's mother. Sue kept flying back and forth to be with her mother for treatments. Then she was reunited with Harvey and, well, they rekindled their romance."

"And when she remarried, she sent the children to live with John?"

"No, when she remarried, she and Harvey headed to Africa for a lengthy honeymoon. He'd always dreamed of using his skills in a developing country where he felt he could make a real difference. Sadly, at some point during their travels, Sue fell ill and never recovered."

"Those poor children."

Bessie nodded. "It's been difficult for them and for John, but Doona does what she can to help. From what I've seen, they're both great kids. They've been invited to tonight's dinner, too."

"I'm looking forward to meeting them. Is there anything else I should know about John or Doona or Hugh or their families?"

Bessie thought for a minute. "I don't think so. I've given you the basics, anyway."

"And that's everyone who will be at dinner tonight?"

"That's everyone from the island who will be there. The others from the cold case unit will be there, too, though."

Matt stared at her for a minute. "Others from the cold case unit? You said 'unit' earlier, but I didn't really think about what you meant. What cold case unit is this, then?"

ALSO BY DIANA XARISSA

The Aunt Bessie Cold Case Mysteries

The Adams File
The Bernhard File
The Carter File
The Durand File
The Evans File
The Flowers File
The Goodman File
The Howard File
The Irving File
The Jordan File
The Keller File

The Isle of Man Cozy Mysteries

Aunt Bessie Assumes
Aunt Bessie Believes
Aunt Bessie Considers
Aunt Bessie Decides
Aunt Bessie Enjoys
Aunt Bessie Finds
Aunt Bessie Goes
Aunt Bessie's Holiday
Aunt Bessie Invites
Aunt Bessie Joins

Aunt Bessie Knows

Aunt Bessie Likes

Aunt Bessie Meets

Aunt Bessie Needs

Aunt Bessie Observes

Aunt Bessie Provides

Aunt Bessie Questions

Aunt Bessie Remembers

Aunt Bessie Solves

Aunt Bessie Tries

Aunt Bessie Understands

Aunt Bessie Volunteers

Aunt Bessie Wonders

Aunt Bessie's X-Ray

Aunt Bessie Yearns

Aunt Bessie Zeroes In

The Isle of Man Ghostly Cozy Mysteries

Arrivals and Arrests

Boats and Bad Guys

Cars and Cold Cases

Dogs and Danger

Encounters and Enemies

Friends and Frauds

Guests and Guilt

Hop-tu-Naa and Homicide

Invitations and Investigations

Joy and Jealousy

Kittens and Killers

Letters and Lawsuits

Marsupials and Murder

Neighbors and Nightmares

Orchestras and Obsessions

Proposals and Poison

Questions and Quarrels

Roses and Revenge

Secrets and Suspects

Theaters and Threats

Umbrellas and Undertakers

Visitors and Victims

Weddings and Witnesses

Xylophones and X-Rays

Yachts and Yelps

Zephyrs and Zombies

The Markham Sisters Cozy Mystery Novellas

The Appleton Case

The Bennett Case

The Chalmers Case

The Donaldson Case

The Ellsworth Case

The Fenton Case

The Green Case

The Hampton Case

The Irwin Case

The Jackson Case

The Kingston Case
The Lawley Case
The Moody Case
The Norman Case
The Osborne Case
The Patrone Case
The Quinton Case
The Rhodes Case
The Somerset Case
The Tanner Case
The Underwood Case
The Vernon Case
The Walters Case
The Xanders Case
The Young Case
The Zachery Case

The Janet Markham Bennett Cozy Thrillers

The Armstrong Assignment
The Blake Assignment
The Carlson Assignment
The Doyle Assignment
The Everest Assignment
The Farnsley Assignment
The George Assignment
The Hamilton Assignment
The Ingram Assignment
The Jacobs Assignment

The Sunset Lodge Mysteries

The Body in the Annex
The Body in the Boathouse
The Body in the Cottage
The Body in the Dunk Tank

The Lady Elizabeth Cozies in Space

Alibis in Alpha Sector
Bodies in Beta Sector
Corpses in Chaos Sector

The Midlife Crisis Mysteries

Anxious in Nevada
Bewildered in Florida
Confused in Pennsylvania

The Isle of Man Romances

Island Escape
Island Inheritance
Island Heritage
Island Christmas

The Later in Life Love Stories

Second Chances
Second Act
Second Thoughts
Second Degree

Second Best

Second Nature

Second Place

Second Dance

BOOKPLATES ARE NOW AVAILABLE

Would you like a signed bookplate for this book?

I now have bookplates (stickers) that I can personalize, sign, and send to you. It's the next best thing to getting a signed copy!

Send an email to diana@dianaxarissa.com with your mailing address (I promise not to use it for anything else, ever) and how you'd like your bookplate personalized and I'll sign one and send it to you.

There is no charge for a bookplate, but there is a limit of one per person.

ABOUT THE AUTHOR

Diana has been self-publishing since 2013, and she feels surprised and delighted to have found readers who enjoy the stories and characters that she imagines. Always an avid reader, she still loves nothing more than getting lost in fictional worlds, her own or others!

After being raised in Erie, Pennsylvania, and studying history at Allegheny College in Meadville, Pennsylvania, Diana pursued a career in college administration. She was living and working in Washington, DC, when she met her future husband, an Englishman who was visiting the city.

Following her marriage, Diana moved to Derbyshire. A short while later, she and her husband relocated to the Isle of Man. After ten years on the island, during which Diana earned a Master's degree in the island's history, they made the decision to relocate again, this time to the US.

Now living near Buffalo, New York, Diana and her husband live with their daughter, a student at the University at Buffalo. Their son is now living and working just outside of Boston, Massachusetts, giving Diana an excuse to travel now and again.

Diana also writes mystery/thrillers set in the not-too-distant future as Diana X. Dunn and Young Adult fiction as D.X. Dunn.

She is always happy to hear from readers. You can write to her at:

Diana Xarissa Dunn
PO Box 72
Clarence, NY 14031.

Find Diana at: DianaXarissa.com
E-mail: Diana@dianaxarissa.com

Made in the USA
Columbia, SC
21 May 2024